In this tale of the 21st century, Arthur Dunn, of Dunn's Clone Catching, Inc., is summoned to Australia by wealthy businessman Sir William Montagu. Dunn must locate Lady Kate Montagu's runaway clone. Lady Kate is very ill; she will die unless her clone can be found in time to provide the vital organ transplants Kate needs to survive.

But Dunn's task is especially difficult, for, like her parent Lady Kate, the Montagu clone is a superb actress. Not only could she be anywhere, but with her talent for theatrical disguise, she could be *anyone*!

Alfred Slote combines an exciting mystery, an action-filled adventure, and a bit of romance in his new novel. The book is illustrated by Elizabeth Slote.

Clone Catcher

by Alfred Slote
illustrated by Elizabeth Slote

J.B. Lippincott   New York

For John Slote and Deborah McDowell

The Clone Catcher
Text copyright © 1982 by Alfred Slote
Illustrations copyright © 1982 by Elizabeth Slote
All rights reserved. Printed in the United States of America.
No part of this book may be used or reproduced in any manner
whatsoever without written permission except in the case of
brief quotations embodied in critical articles and reviews.
For information address J. B. Lippincott Junior Books, 10 East 53rd Street,
New York, N.Y. 10022. Published simultaneously in Canada by
Fitzhenry & Whiteside Limited, Toronto.

Library of Congress Cataloging in Publication Data

Slote, Alfred.
The clone catcher.

Summary: In the twenty-first century Arthur Dunn is
summoned to Australia to track down a runaway clone
urgently needed to provide vital organ transplants for
her parent, the superb actress Lady Kate.
[1. Cloning—Fiction. 2. Mystery and detective
stories. 3. Science fiction] I. Slote, Elizabeth,
ill. II. Title.
PZ7.S635Cl 1982   [Fic]   82–47761
ISBN 0–397–32017–5   AACR2
ISBN 0–397–32018–3 (lib. bdg.)
1 2 3 4 5 6 7 8 9 10
First Edition

Contents

Prologue

"clone"—A group of genetically identical cells descended from a single common ancestor.

> —*The American Heritage Dictionary*, 1979

"If you can clone a plant, you can clone a human being. We are working on it."

> —Prof. V. R. Kolodny— Soviet Academy of Medical Engineering, speech, February 1986

"Human clones are not only scientifically feasible, they may be the only way certain privileged people can afford eternal life."

—Editorial in the *New England Journal of Medicine,* July 1991

"I've just returned from the compound, having visited my clone. I am pleased to report, dear Kate, that it is in excellent health and the very image of me."

—Sir William Montagu of Perth, Australia, in a letter to his wife, April 2004

"Yes, I'm a clone catcher. And good at it. I wouldn't trade the excitement of my work for anything."

—Arthur Dunn, of Dunn's Clone Catching, Inc., in an interview before he left for Australia, November 2019

CHAPTER ONE

Arrival in Australia, November 2019

MY NAME IS ARTHUR DUNN, Dunn's Clone Catching, Inc. Operating out of New York City—fair or foul weather.

Not a pleasant job. Not in the least. Capturing clones is always hard work. But, at the age of twenty-five (old for clone catchers), I'm a professional—and I do my work well enough to charge high prices to those who can afford it.

Sir William Montagu, of Perth, Australia, was one who could afford it. Now in his early seventies, Sir William had amassed a fortune in the gold fields of Australia and Africa.

I received a lasergram from his office telling me only that he needed help in capturing a clone. I promptly took a space shuttle from New York to Satellite Station Austro. There, high above the earth, I was met by a tall, thin, sad-faced man in his early forties.

4

"Norman Montagu," he murmured, and held out a limp hand for me to shake.

The old man's son and heir. From his sad expression it was clear that it was his father's clone that had escaped. Most sons (and heirs) are sorry to see a clone catcher arrive. It usually means they'll have to wait a long time for their inheritance—perhaps forever. (I'll explain more about this later.)

"Arthur Dunn, sir, Dunn's Clone Catching, Inc. At your service," I said quite cheerfully.

"No, no," he protested, "not at *my* service, Mr. Dunn. I shan't pretend that I'm glad to see you, sir."

"No problem, Mr. Montagu," I said, smiling. "I quite understand your point of view in these matters. No grudges held. Shall we get going?"

"Of course," he said.

As I followed Norman Montagu to a space taxi under charter to Montagu Mining Enterprises, I couldn't help reflecting how alike heirs are all over the world. When your father is very rich, as was Sir William, then your principal occupation consists of waiting for him to die so you can inherit his money. It's not a position that strengthens one's manhood.

There was no one else in the space taxi with us except the pilot. Norman Montagu stared gloomily out a porthole as we descended to earth.

The spaceport at Perth was a busy place, with space taxis not only coming and going between it

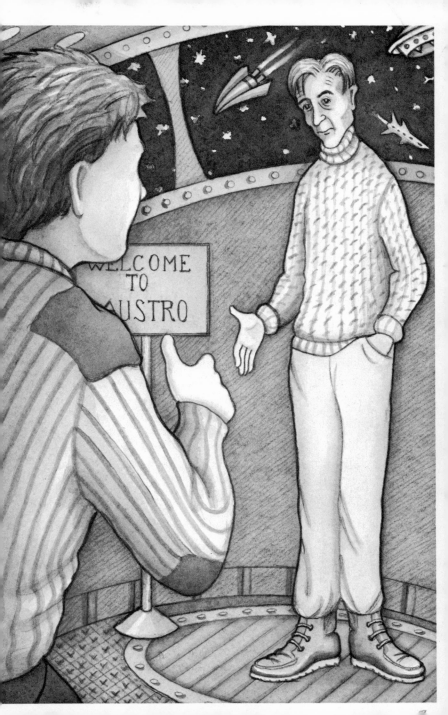

and the satellite station but leaving on local jaunts to other cities in Australia.

My suitcase and passport went through electronic customs via a vacuum tube, while Norman Montagu and I took a VIP elevator to the parking garage on the ground floor of the six-tiered spaceport.

A guard there handed me my suitcase and passport and wished me a pleasant stay in Australia. Pleasant, no, I thought. Successful? I hoped so!

Norman Montagu led me to a beautiful, solar-powered Land Rover.

I congratulated him on owning such a fine vehicle.

"Oh, Father gave it to me for my work," he murmured. "I also take his guests back and forth to Perth in it. Please get in."

I put my suitcase in the back. I didn't have much in it: a change of underwear, a spare shirt, a handkerchief, and my toothbrush. Clone catchers travel light.

Then I got in front with Norman Montagu, though I left myself a bit of room between him and me. This was in case I had to put a karate lock on him. The fact is, more than one clone catcher has been killed by a desperate heir. And quite often, the less violent they look, the more violent they are.

Norman Montagu drove slowly and cautiously through the streets of Perth. And in a few moments we were on a smooth road that ran along the coast. I could hear the surf crashing against the shore of the great Australian continent.

After a dozen or so kilometers the road became

a bumpy dirt track and turned inland, away from the sea.

There were fewer and fewer houses. And finally . . . none.

No signs of human habitation. No lights. Civilization had ended abruptly. We were driving on the edge of the vast Australian desert. A perfect place to murder a clone catcher.

"Lonely country," I said to Norman Montagu, just to let him know I was alert.

"Yes," he said, "I like it."

"Do you? I'd have thought you'd prefer the excitement of Montagu City, the brain cell of your father's great mining enterprises."

(I'd done research on Sir William's business. It behooves a clone catcher to know everything he can about his client's world.)

"Oh," said Norman, "I have nothing to do with my father's business. I live on a small sheep station. Fortunately for me, Father feels I have no head for business."

"Why 'fortunately' for you?"

He smiled sadly. "Because I have none. Nor wish to have one. I like to read books and look after sheep. I think it pleases Father that I am this way. I know it pleases me." He spoke shyly. Was it an act?

"Don't you want to inherit Montagu Mining Enterprises someday?" I asked.

"No, Mr. Dunn. That would be the last thing in the world I would want."

"Then," I asked, "why did you say a while back that you were not pleased to see a clone catcher arrive?"

He looked straight ahead at the dirt track, which looked smooth in the cone of the headlights but was bumpy as the tires went over it.

"Because I dislike people who hunt people," he said.

His tone was sincere. I began to relax.

"As for that, Mr. Montagu," I said, "clones are not people. And it's a mistake to think of them that way."

"In your position I imagine you must believe that," he replied.

"It's not belief, sir," I said flatly, "it's fact."

And that ended our conversation. He seemed harmless. No one for me to worry about. Heir or no heir.

We drove through the endless, dark Australian night and stopped only once—for water at Norman Montagu's sheep station. I watched him fill the car's solar tank with water, and then check on his sheep.

He walked up a small hill behind a barn and I could see him standing near a lone cabbage palm, looking around.

Then he came down the hill, got back in the car, and we drove on toward Montagu City.

"There's so much to worry about on a sheep station," he explained.

"Why live there then?" I asked.

"Because it's peaceful and quiet. All you worry about are sheep."

On a hill and at night? I wondered.

The road turned back to the west, toward the sea, and after about a half-hour it became smooth pavement again. A bluish glow in the sky indicated we were approaching Montagu City.

I saw searchlight beams playing tag among low, dark clouds, and soon the outlines of buildings appeared.

Montagu City was obviously a place of power. It had been built on a headland that jutted out into the Indian Ocean. It was dominated by a huge, sprawling mansion that faced the ocean.

As we approached I saw that this main house was flanked by twin neutro-communication towers. Through these towers Sir William must direct his far-flung mining operations.

Behind the main house, bathed in mercury security lights, I could see several low, modern buildings. I had read the history of Montagu City and studied pictures of the place and knew that these buildings were experimental laboratories. I also saw a chain of research greenhouses lit up inside by purple lights. From *my* research, I knew that Sir William's scientists were working on ways to convert mineral matter to vegetable to help solve food shortages in Africa and in some of the space colonies that surround the earth.

As we drove along the perimeter of the city, I

could see lighted swimming pools and tennis courts set between clusters of homes. I guessed they were for the enjoyment of Sir William's scientists and engineers and their families.

It was a small industro-scientific-recreational city. One would not have to leave it for anything. Indeed, besides Perth, five hours away, there was nowhere else to go.

Past the mansion with its outbuildings, homes, greenhouses, and recreational facilities, I saw a tall, laser-protected wire fence illuminated in the search-light beams.

Here, within the fence, was a second and smaller city that contained cottages and eating, recreational, and educational facilities.

I was impressed with the fence and wondered how it had failed. For failed it had. Or why else had Sir William sent for a clone catcher?

"Here we are," said Norman Montagu, stopping the car in front of the mansion.

CHAPTER TWO

Sir William Montagu

A PRETTY, YOUNG WOMAN greeted us in the entry hall.

"Hello, Norman," she said to Norman Montagu. And then she turned to me, extending a businesslike hand. "And you must be the clone catcher."

I shook her hand. "Arthur Dunn, Miss. Dunn's Clone Catching, Inc."

A faint smile appeared in her cool, green eyes.

"I'm Alice Watson," she said. "And no 'Inc.' about me at all. It was I who sent you the lasergram. I'm the administrator of the main house. I hope you've had a pleasant trip here."

"As trips go, Miss, it was very pleasant."

"You must do a lot of traveling in your job."

"I do."

"Well, I hope you're not too tired. Sir William wants to see you right away. He's in the library."

The library, I thought, is a curious place for a sick man to be.

"Norman, would you take Mr. Dunn to the library? I have to get back to Lady Kate."

She looked at me. "Lady Kate will also want to see you right away. Good-bye for now, Mr. Dunn."

"Good-bye, Miss Watson," I said.

Norman Montagu led me down a wide, carpeted hall. As I followed him, I wondered if they had turned the library into a small hospital. The fact is, if a clone catcher is needed, he is usually sent for when his client is on his last legs. A clone catcher generally follows the doctor's final warning by about eight hours.

Norman Montagu stopped in front of a large, oak door. The initials W. M. were carved by hand in it.

He knocked timidly on the door.

A voice told us to come in.

Norman opened the door cautiously.

We stepped into a large, brown, paneled room. Running the length of one wall was a map. There were light bulbs on the map marking Sir William's mining operations. It was clear that Montagu Mining Enterprises was just about everywhere, and moving into Antarctica.

There were bulbs in outer space that indicated Sir William was mining various asteroids.

Sir William himself sat behind a desk talking into a radio-phone. He was a small, peppery, old man with a shock of white hair and bright, blue eyes. He certainly did not look sick. Nor did he sound sick.

"Of course, we'll buy," he snapped. "We'll buy at any price he wants, but don't tell *him* that. Tell him we won't go over a thousand Swiss francs a ton. And you can have him Vue/Phone me if he doubts your word. He won't doubt my word or my face."

Sir William snapped off the radio-phone without saying good-bye. Always the mark of a leader, I thought.

"What is it, Norman?" He barely masked his irritation.

"The clone catcher is here, Father," Norman said apologetically.

The bright, blue eyes of Sir William Montagu swiveled like twin cannons at me.

"Dunn, is it?"

"Yes, Sir William. Arthur Dunn. Dunn's Clone Catching, Inc. Operating out of—"

"Never mind that. I know all that. The question is: can you find it?"

"I've never failed yet, sir. I have the best track record in the world."

"Of course, you do. That's why I hired you. I only buy the best. But, Dunn . . ." those hard, blue eyes danced maliciously, "you've never been up against a Montagu clone."

I let his challenge pass by. I may be a little fat and look harmless, but I've found it a great advantage in catching clones to look a bit of a fool.

Most clones, you see, are clever. The fact is, only the very rich have been able to get themselves cloned.

And in our twenty-first-century universe, many of the rich tend to be pretty high-powered types. Sir William himself is a good example. And my clients have included people even more powerful than Sir William.

I think of Baron Bugno in Switzerland. A munitions magnate. His clone escaped from a compound near Zurich. I tracked it down to Mexico where it had started a munitions business of its own.

Or the clone of the deputy premier of the Soviet Union—Kirlov. His clone escaped from the clone compound beneath the Kremlin. No easy trick when you think about it. I found Kirlov's clone in Southeast Asia where it was building a military empire there.

As bright and clever as Sir William's clone might be, I had complete confidence in my abilities to track it to the ends of the earth.

The only thing that puzzled me as I stood there facing the little billionaire was why he was in such a hurry to find his clone. He looked in the best of health. And here, perhaps, I'd better explain why my services are in such demand.

CHAPTER THREE

Of Clones and Cloning

WHEN THE SCIENCE OF CLONING began at the end of the 1980s, no one could imagine what practical ends it would eventually serve. But in the year 1991 an article appeared in the *New England Journal of Medicine* that raised the possibility that the human body's rejection mechanism, because of which heart, kidney, liver, lung, and pancreas transplants were never completely successful, could now be overcome if the organs of one's clone were used. Those organs would be an identical genetic match, down to the tiniest, unique cell of the parent, thereby being the perfect transplant.

With the publication of that article it was clear to everyone what the ultimate use of clones would be: living organ banks!

This may sound horrible to some. And, at the time, there were objections by many. Inhuman! they cried. Nobody should live forever! The old must make way for the new!

But in truth, what began to happen (on still a small scale, to be sure) was the new made way for the old!

The young died so that the old could go on living.

There are people today, over 120 years old, living in such pressure-packed cities as New York, Washington, Moscow, and Peking, who are on their second and third set of clone organs.

Eternal life—on earth—is now within one's grasp as long as one's clone organs are available for transplant. The premier of China has three generations of clones living in his compound in Peking. His life, barring accidents or assassination, seems assured for the next two hundred years or so.

The very rich and powerful keep their clones at hand in carefully guarded compounds. Usually out of sight. They are never visited by their "sponsors," for who wishes to become acquainted with someone who must ultimately die for you?

The problem is that no one likes living on borrowed time. (And most attempts to reconcile clones to their purpose in life have failed.) Inevitably, clones, being the bright and resourceful products of their masters' genes, escape from the compound.

And thus has come into our society a new professional—the clone catcher. A job that calls for the skills of a detective and the understanding of a psychiatrist.

It's not a job for everyone. Certainly not for the squeamish. My fees are high—partly as compensation for my ignoring the questionable morality of breeding clones, and partly because I believe anyone who wishes to live forever should pay a stiff price for that dubious privilege.

Although, as I said, Sir William Montagu looked to me to be in perfect health.

I was in for a surprise.

CHAPTER FOUR

A Clone on Stage

SIR WILLIAM CONTINUED: "Montagu clones come from a long line of buccaneers. Tough-minded rascals who would as soon slit your throat as look at you."

"It will indeed be a challenge finding your clone, Sir William," I said.

The blue eyes fired salvos of contempt at me. "Who said anything about *my* clone? My clone is exactly where I left it. Damn it, Dunn, do I look ill to you?"

"No, sir. As a matter of fact, you don't."

"Well, I'm not. I'm seventy-two years old and it will be another twenty years before I'll want my clone's heart." He uttered a short, hard bark of a laugh. By my side, Norman Montagu shifted uncomfortably in his chair.

"It's not my clone I'm wanting, Dunn. It's my wife Kate's. Lady Kate is dying. And her clone is gone."

I stared at him. A female clone! I hadn't known. It made the job that much harder. I should also be charging more.

"When did she escape, sir?"

"She didn't escape, Dunn. She's just gone."

That made no sense to me. You locked up clones. When they were gone it meant they had escaped.

"Gone from where?" I asked.

"Perth," he said.

"Perth," I repeated. "The city of Perth?"

"That's right. What else is Perth but a city?"

"Do you mean to say, sir, that she was kept in Perth?"

This conversation was confusing me. But worse was to come.

"She wasn't *kept* anywhere, Dunn. She was out in the open. On center stage, as a matter of fact."

I hadn't the slightest idea what he was talking about. With all my experience at successful clone catching, I was not at all prepared for what came next.

He picked up a theater program from the top of his desk, looked at it silently for a moment, and then tossed it at me. I caught it and looked at the cover.

There was the picture of an extraordinarily beautiful, young woman. Under the picture it said: SHE STARS IN *TWO TO MAKE MERRY*.

"That's her," Sir William said.

"That's who?"

"The clone, Dunn! The clone!" He was impatient.

"The clone," I repeated, dumbfounded. . . . "The clone is an actress?"

"And a bloody good one, too," Sir William snapped. "Almost as good as Kate in her prime."

I looked at the old man. "Do you mean to say, Sir William, that you permitted Lady Kate's clone to live outside the compound? Without being guarded? That you permitted her to have a career, just as a regular human being might have?"

"That's exactly what I mean to say. That's exactly what I'm telling you. If you don't follow me, Dunn, you're either thick or deaf."

Sir William Montagu had violated the code of behavior that every clone owner agrees to abide by, and far from apologizing for it, he was insulting me.

"You've got to find her and find her fast, Dunn."

Absolutely incredible. I stared at the face on the theater program. Beautiful, and also intelligent and alert.

I looked at the old man. "Do you have any idea where she might be now, sir?"

"If I had 'any idea,' Dunn," Sir William sneered, "I wouldn't need your services now, would I?"

"No, sir."

"The fact is, the police have been scouring Australia for her for the past day and a half. She's disappeared."

And why wouldn't she disappear, I thought. Living unguarded outside a clone compound and knowing that one day her body would be needed.

"When was Lady Kate told she'd need the clone's organs?"

"A week ago."

"And did you then contact the clone?"

"Immediately. And she promised to return here in three days. Her show was to close in three days. Then Kate received a Vue/Phone call from her just two days ago. It was going to be her last performance. Did Kate want to see it? Of course, Kate did. The doctors weren't too happy about her going, but she insisted. I would have gone, too, but . . . but . . . I don't think I could have taken it. . . ." His voice broke. I stared at him. He was embarrassed, red faced. I was beginning to sense something peculiar in the story.

Sir William blew his nose, cleared his throat. "Kate never found her after the performance. She had cleared out. No one saw her go. The police in Perth questioned everyone. Those are all the facts, Dunn."

Not quite all, I thought.

I asked: "When do the doctors want to do the operation on Lady Kate?"

"Immediately," he snapped.

Typical of doctors, who don't have to chase down spare parts. The clone, as I saw it, had a lead on me of at least two days. One could fly to a space colony in less than two days.

Well, there was nothing to do but begin the hunt immediately.

"I'll have to keep this picture," I told him. "And

any other pictures you have of her will be helpful. And any letters, notes . . . I'll need to talk to anyone who knew her."

"*Everyone* knew her," he replied. "Inside the compound as well as here in the main house."

"Then I'll talk to as many as I can. I'll need especially to talk with Lady Kate Montagu."

"Lady Kate wants to talk to you right away. She's been waiting for you anxiously, as you might guess." He hesitated. "Dunn, I'm a little worried about her mental state right now. Living under the threat of the doctor's knife can disturb one's mind. If you know what I mean."

"No, sir. I'm not sure I do know what you mean."

"Kate's tense. She may say strange things. For example, she wanted you summoned. And then this morning she told me to cancel it. She's becoming unhinged. You'll see that for yourself. But mind your manners with her, young man. She may be sick now. But once Kate Montagu was the toast of the world. The greatest actress who ever lived. And I'm including everyone everywhere in that. All right, let's go see her right now."

"Do you want me along, Father?" Norman Montagu asked meekly. I'd practically forgot he was still there.

"No, Norman," Sir William said contemptuously, "you're quite useless. Go back to the sheep station and look after our four-footed friends there."

"Very well, Father."

Norman Montagu bowed himself humbly out of the room, nodding to me just once as he left.

Sir William shook his head and turned to me. "What do you think of Norman, Dunn?"

"It's hard to believe he's your son," I answered truthfully.

"Exactly. That's why cloning is so important, Dunn. There's no such thing as a chip off the old block when two people are involved in the creation of a baby. Too many unknowns can enter into it. Kate was a firebrand, a great woman, a beauty. Her clone is exactly like her. I was no slouch myself— when I performed on the stage or when I prospected for gold. And I finally built an empire of my own. But together, what did Kate and I produce? Norman. Whose greatest ambition is to take care of sheep and read bad novels. How do you account for it, Dunn? I can't. Some hidden DNA lurking in the bushes of the past? No, by God, I won't leave an empire I've built with my own two hands, my own brains and nerve, to a clod like Norman. There's only one person who can continue to run Montagu Mining Enterprises properly—me! That's why I want to live as long as possible, Dunn. I'm not interested in immortality. I want to make sure Montagu Mining Enterprises continues to thrive. That's why I had myself cloned. I needed a supply of spare parts on hand."

"It's too bad you didn't keep Lady Kate's spare parts on hand, too," I said.

He looked at me. "That was different, Dunn. Her clone was . . . beautiful, talented . . . just like her. She—" He searched for words he couldn't find. His voice broke. And then he got angry. "Damn it, Dunn, you do see the problem, don't you?"

I was beginning to. It looked like Sir William Montagu had fallen in love with his wife's spare parts. And now his wife was paying the price.

CHAPTER FIVE

I Meet Lady Kate

SIR WILLIAM OPENED A DOOR in the wall map, right around Antarctica. I followed him through it. We walked down a number of hallways until we reached the residence part of this huge complex. Thereafter we passed through a series of rooms, where I caught glimpses of people working. They appeared to be scientists, engineers, technicians. . . .

Finally we came to another one of those large, oak doors. This at the end of a hallway. The initials K. M. had been carved in it in a beautiful, artistic way.

Over the door was a green light. It reminded me of something but I couldn't think what.

Sir William knocked as timidly on his wife's apartment door as his son, Norman, had knocked on his.

"Kate's a very sick woman," he explained.

There were footsteps on the other side. Then the

door opened. A young nurse stood there in a white uniform. She had a stern, unsmiling face.

"Yes, Sir William?" she asked, without deference.

"Good evening, Fitzimmons. How is Lady Kate this evening?"

"She's resting comfortably, sir," Nurse Fitzimmons said in a clipped tone. She made no move to step aside and let us in.

"Would you tell her that the clone catcher has arrived?"

The nurse looked at me appraisingly. "Yes," she said. "Lady Kate has been waiting for him. Miss Watson told us he had arrived. You may come in. Both of you," she added.

The center hallway of Lady Kate's apartment was decorated with glossy black-and-white pictures of stage sets, stage plays, pictures of movie stars, stage and Vue/Screen personalities, and stars of satellite stage-transmission. All the pictures were autographed: "To Kate and Billy Montagu."

There were many photographs of the woman I understood immediately to be Lady Kate Montagu. It was the same face as the clone's. The face I had seen on the theater program. A handsome, intelligent face with laughing, green eyes.

"Look at her, Dunn!" Sir William said. "The fire in those eyes. And the doctors give her only two weeks. Two weeks, Dunn! It's not fair."

Not to her, I thought, or to me. Two weeks was usually not much time to catch a clone. Especially a female clone. For some reason, female clones are always more successful than male clones at protecting themselves by blending completely into their surroundings.

On the other hand, Lady Kate Montagu was obviously a colorful, dynamic woman. Her clone would have to be the same. And the more dynamic and colorful she was, the easier she would be to find.

"It can be done," I said cautiously.

"It must be done," Sir William said grimly.

We reached another door with another green light above it. Sir William caught my puzzled look.

"It's a stage door," he said. "We transferred it to Kate's apartment. This one was off the Abbey Theatre in Dublin. A gift of the Irish government. The other door was from the Moscow Art Theatre, a gift from the Russians."

We were now in a large room that looked like a stage set. There was a lighting grid overhead with theater lights hanging down from it: spotlights and scoops. The walls were designed to look like theater flats, with trees and buildings painted on them. It was unreal. The theater is supposed to imitate life. But here life was imitating the theater.

Sir William understood my bewilderment. "When Kate could no longer go out," he explained, "we brought the theater to her. I enjoyed doing it. I was once part of the theater myself. I used to be an actor. A good one, too, if I do say so myself. But then I caught a bigger bug—the gold-prospecting bug—and made myself real money. . . ."

He waved his hand at the theater lights, the stage flats. "The stage is gold, Dunn, but it's fool's gold. The real gold is in the land. Or . . ." he looked at me and smiled, "catching clones."

I nodded but said nothing. I make a good living at catching clones. I work hard for my clients. But there is nothing that says I must approve of them or like them.

Nurse Fitzimmons returned. "Lady Kate will see the clone catcher immediately," she said. "But I would advise you both not to stay long. My Lady tires very quickly. And she has been under an emotional strain lately." The nurse's dark eyes looked coldly at me. "She is under a tremendous strain right now."

"I understand, Miss," I said.

And so we moved into another room, and this room was like the front of the stage. But instead of facing out onto an audience, it faced a wide, oval window. Through it I could see the surf crashing against the rocks.

It was as dramatic a room as I'd ever been in. And it matched the presence of the person that Nurse Fitzimmons and Alice Watson now wheeled in.

Lady Kate Montagu was old, but she sat erect, proud, and queenly in her wheelchair. Her face was caked with theater makeup: powder, rouge, lipstick, eye shadow. Red hair rose in piles on her head, and she wore yellow flowers on her dress.

She was beautiful and dreadful all at once.

A clone's spare parts may help you live forever, but they cannot remove the wrinkles from your face, or the age from your hands.

Though someone had done a terrific job on her hands. Lady Kate had long, slender fingers with long, bright red nails. Those fingers beat a nervous tattoo on the metal arms of her wheelchair.

Her voice was deep and harsh.

"Are you the clone catcher, young man?" she demanded.

"Yes, ma'am."

"Stand under the light where I can see you better. I have never seen one of your profession before."

I went and stood under one of the spotlights. She could see me more clearly now, but because the light was now glaring in my eyes, I couldn't see her as well.

"You look," she pronounced, "like a very ordinary man."

"I am a very ordinary man, ma'am."

"An ordinary man will not be able to catch my clone."

Sir William looked uneasy. "Kate," he said, "Mr. Dunn comes highly recommended."

"By whom? Senile, old idiots who have more money than wits and want to live forever?"

Her green eyes glowed at me like an angry cat's.

"Mr. Dunn, I have changed my mind. I don't want to live forever. I've given up this rotten game of life. And you have wasted your time and my husband's money coming here. I say let the clone live her own life. And you, Mr. Dunn, go back to where you came from."

"Now, now, Kate," said Sir William, "you're overexcited. You don't know what you're saying. Why, just two days ago you couldn't wait for me to hire a clone catcher. Now you want to send him packing. No, by God, Kate, we'll find your clone and give you new life."

"You can't give me new life, Billy, you can only give me more of the same old life. I don't want it anymore. I'm tired of it. Let her live and let me die. I want to die now. I tell you, I want to die!"

Tears began rolling down her heavily made-up cheeks.

Sir William was shaken. He was pale. "Kate, no one wants to die, my dear. That's the purpose of cloning. You're acting with me now."

"I'm not acting!" the old woman screamed. "I want to die!"

Sir William looked helplessly at Nurse Fitzimmons and at Alice Watson. But the two of them just stood there without expression.

The old woman sobbed. "All of this could have been avoided if you hadn't permitted her to live like a human being."

Suddenly her tears stopped. She leaned toward me.

"Clone catcher, . . ."

"Yes, ma'am."

"It was *his* fault. His fault that she's gone. His fault that I must die. His fault that I am going out of my mind. His fault, his fault, his fault . . ."

She began weeping again.

"Kate," Sir William pleaded. "Please, Kate, . . ."

"I'll look after her, sir," Nurse Fitzimmons said.

The competent young nurse stepped quickly to Lady Kate's side. In the palm of her hand was a pill. "She'll rest quietly with this."

The old lady took it reluctantly. Those beautiful, old eyes looked at me sadly.

"Go home, clone catcher, and let me die in peace," she whispered.

And then her eyes closed and her head sagged and her breathing became less tortured, then regular and relaxed.

"She'll sleep now," the nurse said.

"Poor darling," Alice Watson murmured, looking sadly at the old woman.

The nurse turned to Sir William and me. Her face was stern. "You both had better leave now. My patient has had enough excitement for one day."

Sir William, pale and shaken, got up and left the room without a word.

The two young women looked at me, waiting for me to leave.

I stood up.

"Sorry to have brought this on just now," I said.

"If there's anything I can do to help . . ."

"Why don't you do what she asked you to do, Mr. Dunn?" Alice Watson said softly. "Go home and let her die in peace. She really doesn't want to live forever."

"Sorry, Miss," I said, "but my client is Sir William. He called me on the case and only he can call me off. I hope that Lady Kate will feel better soon."

"She will," said the nurse coldly, "once you leave."

I left.

CHAPTER SIX

Sad Tale

"I SUPPOSE YOU WANT to know what that was all about," Sir William said to me.

We were back in his library-office with the huge wall map and its blinking lights all over the world.

"Yes, I do."

"I'll turn off the tele-beams so we won't be interrupted. Would you like a drink?"

"No, thank you."

He nodded. "I don't approve of drinking myself. It dulls the mind and the senses and, God knows, we'll need all of that now. Well . . ." He sighed. "Where to begin?" He paused and then turned to the wall map behind him. He pointed to the blinking lights on it. "I started that from nothing, Dunn. Nothing. I didn't inherit Montagu Mining Enterprises—I built it!"

"A great achievement, sir."

He shook his head. "And yet it was nothing. Nothing compared to acting. Nothing compared to illusion. Had I Kate's ability, Dunn, I'd still be acting. Look at how she just performed in her apartment. She wants to die and in the next breath blames me for allowing her clone to escape. Always play-acting until you don't know who you are and what you really want. But in that is greatness, too. I was a poor actor; I hadn't her ability to throw myself into other people's lives. But then, Dunn, one day I found a role that suited me to a T. I became a businessman. And do you know why I did it?"

I shook my head.

"I needed money, Dunn. Money. Kate was having great success all over the world. The only way I could bring her back to Australia was to send private air shuttles. And even then, Dunn, I only got my Kate back two or three times a year."

He looked away from me.

"No wonder," he said softly, "that when her clone was growing up the image of her, I was taken with it. And I wanted it nearby. Not in the compound with the other clones. But here in this house . . ."

He pulled open a desk drawer and took out a picture in a small, silver frame. He handed it to me. I looked at a beautiful, young woman with laughing, green eyes and lovely, red hair that tumbled down around her shoulders.

"The clone?" I asked.

"And Kate, too," he said.

"Kate number two," I repeated, to make sure.

"No," he said, "we called her Mary. Mary Montagu."

"Sir William!"

"I know, Dunn. It's against all the rules of cloning."

"More than that, sir. It's absolutely outrageous. A clone is supposed to be named numerically after its master. Kate Two. Kate Three. Your clone should be William Two."

"And so it is, Dunn. My clone is Billy Two. It wasn't my clone I had a problem with. It was Kate's clone. Look, Dunn, no lectures! You wanted the facts; I'm giving you the facts. We gave Kate's clone— and Kate was as guilty as I was in this—we gave her clone a name of her own. A family name. We treated her as a regular human being."

"An absolutely heartless thing to do, sir!"

"And so it turned out. But at the time we couldn't help ourselves. At the time . . ."

He sat back in his chair and closed his eyes. "Let me start at the beginning, Dunn. . . ."

The beginning took place when Sir William and Lady Kate, both in their fifties, decided to have themselves cloned.

They went to New York City to have it done.

Cells were scraped from the insides of their mouths. Nine months later two babies were airshipped to them with the correct clone names attached: William Two, Kate Two.

Everything proceeded normally until one day, three years later, Lady Kate, returning from filming in England, expressed a desire to see her clone.

"You're not feeling ill, are you, my dear?" asked Sir William.

"No, Billy. I'm just curious."

Sir William could not understand that. He wasn't curious about *his* clone. A clone was a collection of spare parts. You didn't get curious about spare parts.

What Kate wanted, Kate got. He made arrangements for them to receive a tour of the compound in the course of which they were to "accidentally" catch sight of their clones.

The clone compound was being managed beautifully by Archie Three, the clone of Sir William's own Montagu City manager. Both Sir William and Lady Kate were pleased with the educational and social facilities, the quality of the food, the cleanliness of the cottages, the lovely porches that enabled the clones to sit and enjoy the evening air.

All the clones, and there were about seventy of them then, products of Montagu City scientists and engineers, looked healthy and vigorous.

Then they caught sight of Kate Two and Billy Two, both three years old and in a nursery school class.

Billy Two was almost comical with his stubby, bandy legs and pug nose. An early snapshot of his parent. But Kate Two, red hair, freckles, green eyes, was a creature neither Sir William nor Lady Kate could stop staring at. She was beautiful, energetic, intelligent, bold, dramatic. They watched her playing with the other clone children and taking charge of them.

"Why, she's a born actress," Kate said, laughing. "You know, darling, I'd hate to have to compete with her for roles in twenty years."

"You won't have to," Sir William said.

A few days later Kate flew to Paris to act in a musical there. He was always lonely and depressed in the days right after Kate left, and so, to cheer himself up, Sir William sent for Kate's clone.

"It'll be like having a living picture of my Kate around," he told Archie Three. "A miniature."

"It's unheard of, sir," replied Archie Three.

"I don't care if it's unheard of or heard of, Archie Three, send Kate Two to me."

That afternoon Kate Two was delivered to him. He took the little clone walking on the beach and watched her discover the sea. A sea gull flew by and called to them. The little thing listened, laughed, and then imitated the bird's call perfectly. And then she ran along the beach, hopping and skipping and flapping her arms in perfect imitation of the gull's flight.

Sir William was entranced. Reluctantly, he returned the child to the compound that evening. But his spirits were lifted. He was ready to go back to work.

A few days later, after a busy session of gold trading with a South African company, and feeling tired, he sent for Kate Two to have lunch with him. They had a delightful time.

And so it went through that year. He took the clone to Perth to show her the city. He took her to the children's theater there. The child adored it.

It was more of the same the following year during Lady Kate's long absences—a round of jolly visits with little Kate.

When the child was five, he had her moved from the compound and into the house. Archie Three was very upset.

"No good can come of this, Sir William."

"Let me worry about that, Archie," he replied.

Kate, visiting between motion pictures, was as taken with her clone as he was. But she was wary. "Do you think it's wise, Billy, that we get so attached to her?"

"It's no harm, my dear. Soon enough she'll turn into a scrawny, unpleasant adolescent and I'll be more than happy to keep her in the compound."

But the child didn't turn into a scrawny, unpleasant adolescent. She became a delightful, amusing, intelligent, and beautiful, young girl. She was the image of Kate in every way.

And then one day he had her name changed to Mary.

Mary Montagu.

Archie Three begged him not to do it.

"Nonsense," he told Archie Three, "the child has a definite personality of her own. I intend to take care of her education myself."

He enrolled Mary Montagu in an acting school in Perth. She also went to private school in Perth. Everyone adored her. People forgot she was a clone and why clones were bred.

"And I forgot, too," Sir William concluded gloomily. "Archie Three had been correct when he said nothing good could come of it."

"Then Lady Kate's clone has been living here in this house since she was five years old?" I asked.

"No. She lived here, except for schooling in Perth, until she was sixteen."

"And then?"

"Then she moved back to the compound."

I stared at him.

"Why?"

Sir William was silent. Then he shrugged. "It was then that we informed her that she was a clone."

"Do you mean to tell me, Sir William, that not until the clone was sixteen years old was she told her origin?"

"That's exactly what I mean, Dunn. Don't gape at me, man. I've broken every rule in the book and now my Kate is paying for it. If I could undo it I would, but I can't. So I've done the next best thing, I've brought you here. Now enough talk. Get about your business, Dunn. Find Mary Montagu. Bring her back. We'll cut her up and give Kate another twenty or thirty years of life. But no more questions, man. No more past history. What's done is done and cannot be undone."

He pressed a button on his desk. A silent summons to somebody.

It was Alice Watson who appeared. That young woman was everywhere.

"Show Mr. Dunn to his room, Alice."

"One moment, Sir William," I said. "I'll need to speak again with Lady Kate in the morning. Also I'll need to enter the compound and talk with all the clones who knew Mary Montagu."

"I'll take you to the compound myself," Sir William said, without looking at me.

Alice Watson showed me to a magnificent guest room on the floor above. It overlooked the ocean. My suitcase was already there.

"Is there anything special you might be needing now, Mr. Dunn?" Miss Watson asked.

"No, Miss. I'm impressed with how efficient everyone is. And how many duties you seem to have. You're just about everywhere."

"I do my best," she said.

"Whom *do* you work for? Sir William or Lady Kate?"

"I work for the Montagu family, Mr. Dunn," Alice Watson replied, a faint smile in her beautiful eyes.

"And does that include Mary Montagu, Miss?"

"Only if you include clones in the family. Most people don't. But then a clone catcher might operate differently. Good night, Mr. Dunn."

"Miss Watson, . . ."

"Yes, Mr. Dunn?"

"I prefer to prepare my own breakfast, if it's all right with you."

She looked amused. "Don't you trust our cook, Mr. Dunn?"

"I don't know your cook, Miss. But I haven't lived as long as I have by trusting people I don't know."

"How old are you, Mr. Dunn?"

"Twenty-five."

"Oh. Is that old for a clone catcher?"

"It's a dangerous profession, Miss."

"Why do it then?"

"I enjoy the dangers."

"And it doesn't bother you to catch people who will ultimately be killed?"

"I don't think of them as people, Miss."

"What *do* you think of them as?"

"Clones."

"What is a clone, Mr. Dunn?"

"A product of a single cell, Miss."

"That looks, acts, thinks, feels like a human being. Isn't that also right?"

I looked at her directly. "How would you know that, Miss?"

Alice Watson looked right back at me. "Living near a clone compound, I have a good idea what clones are like."

"May I ask you a question now, Miss?"

"Of course."

"How old are *you?*"

She hesitated just a fraction of a second. "Twenty-five," she said.

"And Mary Montagu? How old would she be?"

Alice Watson looked toward the window and the dark ocean that raged outside.

"I believe Mary is nineteen."

"You two must have been close."

She smiled. "We were friends. Will there be anything else, Mr. Dunn?"

"Not now."

"Then, good night, Mr. Dunn."

"Miss Watson!"

She paused at the door.

"You wouldn't happen to know where Mary Montagu is, would you?"

I asked it casually, almost as an afterthought. She smiled and said: "No, Mr. Dunn. I wouldn't know."

She closed the door behind her. Extraordinary woman, I thought.

I unpacked my small suitcase. I wondered if I'd brought enough clothes. My guess was that I hadn't. That I'd be staying in Australia longer than I'd planned.

CHAPTER SEVEN

"Let Her Die!"

UNFORTUNATELY, for someone who travels a lot, I've never been able to sleep well in strange beds. That night I was more uncomfortable than ever. Perhaps it was the sound of the ocean crashing against the rocks. Perhaps it was the memory of Sir William's strange and sad tale.

To give a clone a human name. To treat it as a human being, giving it the hopes and dreams of a human being, and then to hunt it down for its parts— this was most inhuman.

Nevertheless I had a job to do for these people. Nor did I think that Lady Kate's clone would be very difficult to catch. If she was as bold as she was beautiful, she would be giving herself away somewhere.

But where?

I fell asleep toward dawn and awoke soon after to a knock at my door.

"Who is it?"

"Cook, sir. With your breakfast. Lady Kate will talk with you in a half-hour."

I opened my eyes. The sun was streaming through the windows. I'd slept longer than I'd thought.

"Come in," I said.

A cheerful-looking, robust woman in a kitchen uniform came in pushing a cart loaded with dishes.

"Top of the morning to you, sir," she greeted me. "I've got a nice, hearty breakfast for you."

She began taking covers off the dishes.

"It's very nice of you, cook," I said, "but I told Miss Watson that I'd prepare my own breakfast."

"Oh, we can't have that, sir. Not here. It wouldn't be very hospitable of us, would it? I told Miss Watson that, and she said, 'All right, cookie, then you bring the breakfast yourself to Mr. Dunn, so if he's poisoned he can lay his hands on you himself.' " The cheerful woman laughed heartily.

I smiled. "Miss Watson is very clever."

"Oh, she's got a head on her, that one. What's your favorite breakfast now? Eggs, pancakes, cereal, perhaps all? I've cooked it all for you. I know Americans like big breakfasts. . . ."

While she prattled on, I examined the food. The orange juice had the right color. The cereal smelled okay. The eggs—I recalled that a clone catcher operating in England had been poisoned by poached eggs. Although these eggs were fried sunnyside-up, I decided to pass them up.

And then there were the pancakes. I examined

the stack, turning over each cake carefully. A clone catcher in Argentina once had found ground glass in his pancakes.

"Something wrong with the cakes, sir?" the cook asked anxiously.

"Not yet."

"Have lots of enemies, have you?"

"And not too many friends."

There was something odd about the bottom pancake. I had difficulty turning it over. When I finally did, I saw why. Something was sticking to the plate. I scraped off a small piece of thin, white cardboard. On it was a message—three typed words: LET HER DIE!

I held the piece of cardboard up. "Do you write as well as cook, Miss?"

The cheerful cook squinted at my hand. "Sir?"

"You didn't happen to slip a note into my pancakes, did you?"

"A note in your pancakes, sir?" Either she was truly astonished or I was in the presence of another actress.

"That's right. A note in my pancakes."

"I've never heard of such a thing and I've been making pancakes for forty years."

"Who else was in the kitchen with you this morning?"

"Sir William. He eats there every morning with Miss Watson. They go over business matters. And the nurse was there, too. Getting tea for poor Lady Kate."

"It sounds like a traffic jam in the kitchen."

The cook laughed, relieved that I wasn't upset. "Oh, it's a rather big kitchen, sir."

"Would you like to see the message on this note?"

"I don't have my reading glasses, sir."

"It says: 'Let her die!' "

"Oh, dear," The cheerful woman looked upset. "Let who die, Mr. Dunn?"

"I was about to ask you that, cook. Let who die? Lady Kate or her clone?"

"Well, I'm sure I don't know the answer to that. I'm only the cook here. As for me, I hope nobody dies in Montagu City. Isn't that why Sir William has such a big clone compound?"

I tasted a bit of the pancake. It was delicious.

"Tell me, cook, does everyone in Montagu City have a clone?"

"Oh, no, Mr. Dunn. Just the important people: the managers, scientists, engineers. . . ."

"What about the cooks?"

She laughed. "Well, I think not. Though a good cook isn't so easy to find these days. How do you like the cakes?"

"Excellent."

She looked pleased.

"Would you like to have a clone of your own, cook?"

The good woman thought about it. "I think not, sir."

"Why not?"

"I think when my time comes to die, why I'd

48

just like to die."

"Do you think others should feel that way?"

"Oh, no, sir. What others do is their business. Right?"

I nodded. "What about the clone Mary Montagu? Did you know her?"

"Oh, right well, sir. We all did. Everyone was very fond of Miss Mary. She was a dear. Would you like me to put an egg on your cakes?"

"No, thank you. I'm doing just fine. What was really so nice about Mary Montagu, cook?"

"Well, she was cheerful. And you can't have too many cheerful people about, I say. And bright. And spunky. Very spunky."

"Would you say she was the type to fight back or run away?"

"From what?"

"Having her body cut open for her organs."

The cook closed her eyes. A shudder went through her body.

"I don't know, sir. That's a terrible thing they do to those clones. That's why I avoid the compound. Never look through the gate."

"Having Miss Mary about the house must have been hard on you."

"Tell you the truth, Mr. Dunn, with Miss Mary you forgot she was a clone. I think Sir William and Lady Kate forgot, too."

"How long did she live in this house?"

"Oh, sir. I don't know. Till she was sixteen about."

"And then?"

"She went back to the compound."

"Did they send her back?"

"Oh, no. He wouldn't. But Miss Mary insisted."

"Why?"

"I guess she wanted to be with her own kind."

"Did that surprise you?"

"No. Miss Mary was that sort of person. She wasn't afraid of anything. Not a thing. Spunky. Yes, spunky is the word for her."

"After she went back to the compound, did you ever see her again?"

"Oh, many times."

"You visited the compound?"

"No, sir. I stayed as far from that compound as I could. She would visit here."

"Could she leave the compound freely?"

"Yes, sir."

"Did she visit here often?"

"Not often enough to suit *him.*"

"You mean Sir William?"

"Aye." I detected a tinge of bitterness there.

"So Miss Mary Montagu, Lady Kate's clone, lived either here or in the compound then?"

"Well, I understand she had an apartment in Perth, too. She performed there on the stage. Just like Lady Kate once had. Sir William used to go in regularly to see her performances."

"Did you go?"

"No, sir. I'm not fond of play-acting."

"Do you know her address in Perth?"

"No, sir."

"Do you have any idea where she is now, cook?"

"No, sir."

"Would you tell me if you did?"

The good woman looked troubled. "I don't properly know that I would, sir."

"I appreciate your honesty, cook."

"It's not that, sir. It's that like everyone else I love Miss Mary."

"What about Lady Kate? Don't you love her, too?"

The cook was silent a moment. "Yes, sir," she said reluctantly.

"Who sent that note to me, cook?"

"I don't know, sir."

I gave her a hard look. "If I'd eaten that piece of cardboard I'd have got indigestion."

She beamed. "I assure you, sir, we have an excellent medical staff in Montagu City."

"What about your reputation as a cook?"

She laughed. "Oh, they'd forgive a slip once in a while."

She wheeled her cart out the door. I wondered why Alice Watson had sent her to me.

CHAPTER EIGHT

I Surprise the Ladies

SEATED ON A SUN DECK overlooking a now more gentle ocean, I found a different Lady Kate Montagu from the one of last evening. This lady Kate was as calm as the ocean. The medicine had done wonders. By her side sat Nurse Fitzimmons, alert, and distrustful of me.

"I won't be too long," I assured the nurse.

"No," said Lady Kate imperiously, "you may take as long as you like. I feel much better this morning. Don't I, Fitzimmons?"

"Yes, my lady."

"Last night I felt dreadful. And I was a bad hostess, Mr. Dunn. I want to say now how much I appreciate your coming all the way from New York to locate my ungrateful clone. Now, please ask your questions."

"Do you have any idea where your clone is, ma'am?"

"That is a very stupid question, young man. If I knew where she was, would we have sent for you?"

Her eyes flashed angrily. Nurse Fitzimmons gave me a warning look. I was driving up her blood pressure.

I nodded. "Well, ma'am," I said mildly, "in the course of clone catching I've run into many strange situations. People play all kinds of games with themselves and with me, too."

"I am not playing a game, Mr. Dunn," Lady Kate snapped, "unless you consider dying a game."

"I don't, ma'am. Could you tell me then when and where you last saw your clone?"

Lady Kate closed her eyes. The sun was bright and warm on all of us. The ocean murmured below. Gulls flew by, their wings tipping the water. A strong-flying pelican flew by about a hundred feet offshore.

"The last time I saw Mary was three nights ago. She was performing in *Two to Make Merry*. I was in the audience."

"Was this after she knew her body was needed by the doctors?"

She looked at me.

"Yes. It was also the last performance of the play. She invited me to see it and said she would return to Montagu City with me. I liked the idea of going to see her in it." Lady Kate smiled at me. "It was a role I'd performed many years ago in London. I wanted to see how Mary would do it. She did it magnificently. As good as I. Even better. Do you like the theater, Mr. Dunn?"

"I don't have much time for it, ma'am."

"Make time for it!" Lady Kate snapped. "The theater is important! It brings joy to people, releases them from their everyday cares. That's why Billy and I put a theater in the compound. The theater, Mr. Dunn, is—"

It was clear she was going to run on a bit about the theater, so I interrupted her.

"Ma'am, can we return to three nights ago? Your clone did not come back to Montagu City with you, did she?"

The excitement drained from the old lady's face. Sad lines carved themselves into her makeup.

"No, Mr. Dunn, she did not. Nurse Fitzimmons and I went backstage and waited for Mary outside her dressing room. Didn't we, Nurse?"

"Yes, my lady," the nurse said.

"We waited and waited and waited, Mr. Dunn," Lady Kate went on. "But Mary never came out of her dressing room."

"Was there another exit from it?"

"No. I don't believe so."

"Is it possible she never returned to her dressing room?"

"I suppose it is."

"Did any of the other members of the cast see her?"

"The police asked that right away. But there was

such a good deal of coming and going backstage.
It was the last performance. There was to be a cast
party, and all that sort of thing."

"Is the play a modern play?"

Her fine, green eyes fixed on me. "What are you
getting at, Mr. Dunn?"

"Would she be wearing modern clothes on stage?
Could her stage clothes also be traveling clothes?"

"Of course, they would be."

"Then she simply walked out a side door, a stage
door, and escaped."

Lady Kate was silent. "Perhaps," she said softly.
"But why would she do that to me, sick as I am?
She was so loyal to me. And I trusted her. We permitted her to live outside the compound. She knew
what her real role was. Her real-life role. How could
she have denied her responsibilities toward me?"

This was more like a typical client, I thought.
Spoiled and selfish.

I answered politely: "Clones can do a good many
things, ma'am, when their lives are at stake. And
when you give them human names and let them
lead normal human lives, then you're also giving
them a big stake in living."

"That," she said flatly, "was William's idea."

"But you went along with it."

"She was such a charming little thing."

"You should have kept her a *thing.*"

"Hindsight, Mr. Dunn. Hindsight."

"Hindsight is better than no sight, ma'am."

"But it doesn't solve our problems. The question is: what are you going to do?"

"I'm going to find your clone, ma'am. That's certain."

"You're very confident."

"I've never failed yet. Lady Kate, if you were afraid for your life where would you go?"

Those beautiful, green eyes looked away from me, toward the gentle sea, its swells, the white birds skimming over its waves.

"Far away, Mr. Dunn. I'd go very far away."

"Where to?"

"America. South Africa. Perhaps England or Ireland."

"And what would you do there?"

"What I do everywhere. The only thing I know to do. Act. Perform. On one stage or another. I would act offstage, too." She looked at me. "I would have to do that, wouldn't I, Mr. Dunn?"

"Yes, ma'am, you would. You'd have to take a different name. What kind of name would you take?"

She thought about that a moment. And then smiled. "I'd take a name from a play. A name quite different from Mary. I'd take a long, romantic name. Amanda, perhaps."

"Would you get involved with a man?"

Laugh crinkles emerged around her eyes. "Many men, darling," the old, harsh voice chuckled. "But I would be true to only one. For that is my nature. Isn't it, Mr. Dunn?"

"I believe it is, ma'am."

"But why do you ask me what *I* would do, Mr. Dunn? How is that helpful to you?"

"You are your clone, ma'am. And she is you. When I talk to you I talk to her. I hunt her by hunting you. This is the secret to successful clone catching. Catch the parent, catch the clone. And that is why I was not as upset as Sir William was last night when you asked me to call off the hunt, because it is really a hunt for you. Have no fear, ma'am. I will only drop my search on orders from Sir William who is, in fact, my employer of the moment."

"Amazing," Lady Kate exclaimed. "You are an amazing man, Mr. Dunn."

"One final question, ma'am. And then I have to visit the compound. Your clone, Mary . . . would you call her 'spunky'?"

Lady Kate's eyes probed mine. "Spunky?" she repeated. "Meaning what?"

"Would Mary run or fight if she were in trouble?"

Lady Kate smiled. The wrinkles around her eyes and lips deepened.

"Actors don't fight, Mr. Dunn. Actors change, take different roles. Mary would leave to perform on a different stage, a stage where she could be free. She's far from here, Mr. Dunn. And every moment you stay here, she gets farther and farther away. Sinking into an obscure role in an obscure city . . ."

"Thank you, ma'am. I'm off to the compound now. I hope to have more definite news for you by this evening."

Lady Kate and the nurse looked surprised.

"So soon?" Lady Kate asked. "Then you think you know where she is?"

"Yes, ma'am. The question will be identifying her, not finding her. Good day to you, ladies."

I left them quite surprised. But not, I hoped, shocked. That would come later.

CHAPTER NINE

The Compound

I FOUND SIR WILLIAM in the front hall conferring with Alice Watson.

"I'll be with you in a moment, Dunn," he said.

Miss Watson was dressed in a brown sweater and green skirt. She looked both businesslike and beautiful. She held a clipboard and pencil, and was taking notes as Sir William spoke.

He was giving her directions about lasergrams to be sent to mine managers in Africa. He also gave her orders concerning various sheep stations in Australia.

Although he looked tired, Sir William's voice was businesslike. Finally, he finished with her and turned to me.

"All right, Dunn, come along now. We'll get over to the compound."

He stomped out the door. I lingered behind.

"I'd like to talk to you a moment, Miss," I said to Alice Watson.

"Ordinarily I'd be delighted to talk with you, Mr. Dunn. But I'm very busy this morning."

"I didn't know you managed Sir William's sheep stations, too."

"I do. Now, if you'll excuse me—"

"I suppose you manage the one Norman Montagu lives on."

"I keep the accounts for it, if that's what you mean. I really don't have time now, Mr. Dunn."

"That was an interesting cook you sent to me this morning, Miss. Especially when I had planned on making my own breakfast."

"You wouldn't have had time to make your own breakfast and still talk with Lady Kate," Alice Watson said. "I do hope . . ." a faint smile curled her lips, "that the breakfast tasted all right."

"Delicious. Especially some interesting pancakes."

"Cook is a wonderful pancake maker. I'll see you later, Mr. Dunn."

"One moment, Miss."

"Sir William will be annoyed with you, Mr. Dunn."

"I'll take that risk. I was wondering how long you've been working here."

"I really must get to work."

I blocked her way and repeated my question.

She sighed. "A few months."

"Were you specially trained for this work, Miss?"

"Why? Do you think I'm doing a bad job, Mr. Dunn?"

"Not at all, Miss. But it seems to me you have a good deal of power here for one so young and so new to Montagu City."

"No more power than you have, Mr. Dunn, for one so young and so new to Montagu City."

"I'm just a clone catcher, Miss."

"Just a clone catcher," she repeated, with a bitter smile. "Is that all? Just a mere man with power of life and death. Run along, Mr. Dunn . . ." she said with contempt, "Sir William is waiting."

I looked out the hall window. Sir William was now on the path that led to the compound.

"I'll see you later today, Miss."

"I'm always here, Mr. Dunn."

Did I sense a mocking tone in her voice?

No matter, I had to run. And run I did, catching up with my client as he marched along between a row of tall Australian pines. Ahead of us loomed the huge, laser-protected fence.

Sir William glanced at me as I came puffing up.

"What kept you, Dunn?" he asked.

"I . . . uh . . ." I was getting my breath back. It's a good thing we clone catchers use our heads and not our legs to catch clones. I was truly out of shape.

Sir William was amused. "The girl attracts you, does she?"

She . . . has beautiful eyes, sir."

"Eyes," he snorted. "You're not here to fall in love with beautiful eyes, Dunn."

"I'm not in love, sir. I'm just curious about Miss Watson."

"Well, stop being curious about Alice. She's a friend of Mary's. Best thing I ever did was hire her. She came in from Perth with a letter from Mary. I hired her on the spot. Reminded me of Mary. Clever. Never has to be told anything twice. Kate's crazy about her, too. All the managers like her." His blue eyes gleamed maliciously. "And I guess you like her, too."

"I'm a clone catcher, sir," I said reprovingly.

"Is that so? And don't clone catchers ever fall in love, Dunn?"

"Not on the job, sir."

Sir William barked a laugh. Ahead of us through the fence I saw the cottages and buildings of his compound. It was beautifully landscaped with pools and fountains and shrubs, walking and running paths. Sir William had spent a great deal of money to make his clone compound a delightful place to live.

"You approve, Dunn?" he asked me.

"Quite, sir. It is very attractive."

"Ever seen a nicer one?"

"No," I answered truthfully. "And I've seen a good many, sir."

He looked at me curiously as we approached the

main gate. The guards in the control towers saluted him and prepared to set in motion the machinery that would open the heavy gate.

"How'd you get into the clone-catching business anyway, Dunn?"

"I was a policeman in New York, sir. The commissioner's clone escaped. I caught it. Pretty soon I was transferred to the clone squad. After that I saw I could make more money catching clones freelance than working for the city."

"I can believe that," Sir William said. "Have *you* been cloned, Dunn?"

"No, sir."

"Why not?"

"It's a bit on the expensive side for me, sir."

"I don't believe that. Not with the prices you charge."

"Oh, I could afford to have a clone made, sir, but keeping it is another story."

He nodded. "I know about that all right. Well, I've learned my lesson. You find Mary and I'll never make a mistake like that again. Dunn, before we go in . . . tell me the truth. How was Lady Kate this morning?"

"Much better than last night, sir. Calm."

He looked relieved. "Last night was bad. I deserved everything she said. Well, you find Mary. Get me off the hook, Dunn. Find that clone. If you don't, I'll lose my Kate forever."

"I'll find the clone, sir."

"Soon, Dunn, soon. If she looks better this morning, she can also be at death's door by evening."

"I expect to find the clone within a few hours, sir."

Sir William looked startled. "Do you have any leads?"

"A few, sir. But none I'd like to talk about now."

He understood that. He was a businessman himself.

"Let's go in," he said.

The gate was opened. Across from us, inside the compound, standing next to a large, heart-shaped pool, stood a tall man wearing a cape and hat. He was an odd, dramatic figure and, dressed that way, it took me a moment to realize he was a clone.

Clones are, at first glance, indistinguishable from normal people. But when you've been around them a bit you see the differences. Their skin has a taut, waxy look, as though it were somehow pulled tight. I understand this may be due in part to their being created from a single cell. It might also be the result of their being brought up without parents and living most of their lives in a state of tension, in guarded compounds. A creature that has never known freedom usually looks different from those who have.

The tall, oddly dressed clone bowed as we entered the compound.

"A pleasure to welcome you here, Sir William," the clone said.

"Good morning, Archie Three. Archie, this is Mr.

Dunn, a professional clone catcher from America. Archie manages the compound for me just as his parent, Archie Thompson, manages one division of my mining enterprises for me. Archie, Mr. Dunn's come here to find Mary."

Archie Three bowed to me. Polite and controlled. A well-mannered clone, I thought.

"We shall, of course, do all we can to help you, Mr. Dunn. This is the first time anyone has been missing. I personally find this very disturbing. I can assure you that you will receive full cooperation from all of us."

Like most clones he avoided using the word "clone." It was a hard life they had with death constantly on the doorstep.

"Thank you," I replied. "I'll need to talk to everyone who knew the clone called Mary Montagu. Starting with Sir William's own clone."

Sir William was surprised. "Billy Two? You want to talk to Billy Two?"

"Yes, sir. He'll be a clue to where Lady Kate's clone is right now."

Sir William, being a normal human being, didn't understand that. But Archie Three, being a clone, immediately understood.

"All right," Sir William growled, "let's get hold of Billy Two. Where is he, Archie?"

"In the social hall, sir. They're rehearsing a play. If you'll come with me, gentlemen."

We followed Archie Three around the heart-shaped pool. It really wasn't a swimming pool. It was a decorative pool; at the bottom of the blue water were hundreds of thousands of white pebbles.

"Kate's idea," Sir William said. "She wanted something beautiful to counteract the guard control towers when one entered. What's this, Archie?"

Archie Three suddenly stopped, and so did we. Coming toward us, on a cinder running path, were six or seven pale, young male clones. They wore brightly colored sweatsuits; they were running, swinging their arms, and singing as they ran.

> One, two, three, four,
> Everywhere but out the door.
> Five, six, seven, eight,
> We don't mourn our fate.

And on past us they ran, running easily while they sang. They were obviously in superb condition.

"Whose clones are they, Archie?" asked Sir William.

"Middle management's, sir. And one or two belong to some of your engineers in Africa."

"A fine lot, aren't they, Dunn? Fit as fiddles. A sight to cheer one's heart, Archie."

"Thank you, sir."

Sir William gestured toward the small, white cottages with their neatly tended gardens, the tennis courts, and cricket field. "People said I was mad to give clones facilities like these—better than normal people's. But, Dunn, that's the least I could do for them."

"Very true, sir. And it keeps their bodies in top shape."

"That's the beauty of the scheme, Dunn. Do for others and you do for yourself. I've followed that rule in business and it's one reason I've been so successful."

"What are those small, square buildings behind the cottages, Sir William?"

"Squash courts. So they can stay in shape in winter when they can't run, or play tennis or cricket."

"And those long, low buildings there?"

"Library/classroom building. A healthy mind makes for a healthy body, Dunn. That building there is our infirmary. First-class medical facility. There's the dining room past the social hall."

"And the tower, Sir William?" I asked.

I was curious to see his response to this. It was obvious what the tower was. Every clone compound has one. This tower was directly in the middle of the compound, about two hundred yards from the main gate. It was a true symbol, a warning. I wanted to know the kind of label Sir William put on it.

"Dunn, you know as well as I do what that is. Some call it the Re-education Center, some call it Rest and Meditation. I call it what it is: the 'slammer.' Anybody in the 'slammer' now, Archie?"

"No, sir. Completely empty."

"As you see, Dunn, we don't use it much. Our

clones are a happy lot. We don't have many radicals around. The top floor is the solitary cell. If a clone attacks a guard or a doctor or a parent coming in to check on it, into solitary it goes. But I can't think of the last time solitary was occupied. Can you, Archie?"

"No, sir."

"It's a first-class compound, Dunn. Don't you agree?"

"Absolutely, sir. A model compound."

It was, too. As we followed Archie Three through the compound toward the social hall where we'd find Sir William's clone, I mapped the whole of it in my head. Later I drew this crude map:

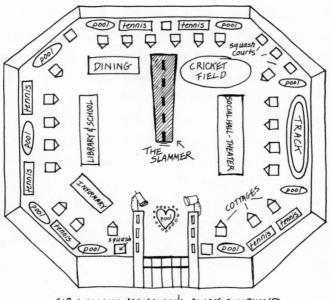

SIR WILLIAM MONTAGU'S CLONE COMPOUND

As you can tell, I'm no artist. But even from my map you can see the good sense of the compound. It consisted of ovals within ovals. The outermost oval was the big, laser-protected fence. Inside that, a series of athletic facilities: tennis courts, squash courts, swimming pools, and a running track. Within that oval were the small, lovely cottages, each of which had a porch on which the clones could sit and take the evening air. Then came the central area, which contained the infirmary, library and school, the dining hall, the social hall/theater, the cricket field, and, in the middle, the tower that Sir William bluntly labeled the "slammer."

Well designed, with care, imagination, and money. I admired it sincerely.

The social hall/theater that we now entered was especially impressive. Very few clone compounds had theaters, but naturally with Sir William and Lady Kate's interest in the theater, their compound would have a first-rate one.

Archie Three led us into a large, darkened auditorium with a stage at one end. Past the auditorium was another large area for dancing and indoor games, such as Ping-Pong and badminton.

"We can pull out a divider here so the theater can be in use at one end while a badminton game is going on at the other. What do you think of that, Dunn?"

"Impressive, sir."

"Shsh . . ." someone whispered from a seat.

On the stage, actors were rehearsing a play. We walked toward them. I could see right away which actor was Sir William's clone. Billy Two was short, red headed, and bandy legged. A younger mirror of Sir William.

We watched Billy Two advance to the center of the stage. He was going to make a speech toward an audience of mostly empty seats.

"This land is our land," he shouted out. "They brought us here in chains. We built this land for them. And now we'll destroy it." He turned to the others. "Destroy!" he yelled.

"Destroy," the others on stage repeated.

"Not bad at all," Sir William whispered. "Billy Two performs a little better than I used to."

"What kind of a play is this?" I asked Archie Three.

"It's about the beginning of Australia," Archie Three replied. "Our country, as you may know, was founded by convicts from England."

"Oh."

On the stage another actor said to Billy Two: "But they don't know what they've done to us."

BILLY TWO: "It doesn't matter whether they know or not. They are agents of evil and must be destroyed!"

OTHER ACTOR: "You don't know what you're saying. They'll kill us all first."

BILLY TWO: "They're killing us by inches anyway. We have nothing to lose but our lives, which are already lost. I say: destroy! Destroy!"

EVERYONE ON STAGE: "Destroy! Destroy! Destroy!"

Their sounds echoed into silence.

And then the lights went on.

"Who wrote this play?" I asked Archie Three.

"I believe it was Miss Mary who wrote it for the clone theater," Archie Three said.

"That girl could do everything," Sir William said, admiringly, missing the point of the whole thing.

"This play must not be permitted to go on," I told Sir William. "It's really an appeal to revolt."

"Nonsense," Sir William said. "You heard Archie. It's about the founding of Australia. We can't stop the theater. Kate's crazy about the clone theater. It's one of her few joys. Archie, get Billy Two over here."

"Billy Two," Archie Three called out, "you have visitors here."

But Billy Two had already seen us. And he was glaring at us with those same hard, blue eyes of his parent.

"I'm coming," he snapped.

He jumped off the stage and came stomping over to us. A younger, stiffer replica of his father. His face was tense. His whole body was taut with suppressed anger.

"What do *you* want here?" Billy Two said to his parent.

"A little help from you, lad," Sir William said

mildly. "Mr. Dunn here is a professional clone catcher. Come all the way from America. I've hired him to find Mary. He wants to talk with you about her. Dunn, . . ."

"Just a few questions about you and—"

That was as far as I got. I saw his fist coming but because it was an unmotivated move on his part I wasn't really prepared for it.

I ducked but his fist caught me on the side of my face.

Down I went.

And out.

CHAPTER TEN

The "Slammer"

THERE ARE HAZARDS in any profession. Pilots crash, sailors drown, and clone catchers get bashed in the head.

Usually I can tell when I'm about to be attacked, and being an expert in the martial arts, I can pretty well handle myself and my attacker. But for some reason Billy's hitting me at that moment was out of character. It was logical that he would hate me. Because of his genetic makeup, he would have to be in love with Mary Montagu. But his hitting me at that moment, I sensed, was *not* a hot-blooded act. There was something very calculated about it.

When I woke up, I saw two faces peering down anxiously at me. Sir William and Archie Three.

Someone had put a pillow under my head.

"Thank goodness," Sir William said. "For a second I thought my lunatic clone had killed you."

"Not quite," I mumbled. I touched my face. It

was puffy and sensitive. I took out my handkerchief and gently dabbed it. No blood. That was good. Billy Two owed me a return engagement.

"Where is he?" I asked, sitting up.

"Who?"

"Billy Two."

"He's in the 'slammer' where he belongs," Sir William snapped. "In solitary! I don't tolerate that kind of behavior around here."

I rose to my elbows, leaning on Archie Three for support. My head was feeling better every second.

"Let's go there. I still want to talk to him."

"Are you mad? He'll kill you. He wanted to kill you."

"No, he didn't. He had another purpose in mind."

"What purpose?"

"I don't know yet, Sir William. That's one of the things I want to find out."

"Well, I won't let you see him alone," Sir William said. "I'll have a guard go into solitary with you."

"No," I replied, "I want to talk with your clone alone. And don't worry about him beating me up again. It won't happen again."

"Are you sure?"

"Positive."

The central area of the compound had filled with tense and upset clones: old and young, male and female. They were agitated. Word had got out that a clone catcher had arrived and that Billy Two had struck him.

Several clones were standing at the base of the "slammer," looking up toward the top window, gesturing, talking among themselves.

"They won't be able to see him," Sir William said. "I installed a one-way mirror-window up there a long time ago. A prisoner can see out but no one can see in. That way we won't have any politicking from the 'slammer' or . . ." he looked meaningfully at Archie Three, ". . . from the ground either."

Archie Three cleared his throat. He clapped his hands. He addressed the agitated mass of clones. "All of you now, please disperse. You children should be in your classes now. You others, why aren't you back on the tennis courts, or in a swimming pool. The library is open. The social hall is open. There's a cricket match scheduled for this afternoon. There is no need to stand around and upset yourselves. Everything is going to be all right. Disperse, please!"

But the clones stayed where they were—staring at us, pointing to me, and looking angrily at Sir William.

A small, young male clone detached himself from a group of other child clones and walked up to us. The clone could not have been more than six or seven years old. He pointed to me. "Archie," he asked in a high, piping voice, "is he the one who's come to catch Mary?"

Archie's face reddened. Sir William frowned. His model clone compound was model only on the surface. Beneath the surface things were very wrong indeed.

I bent down so that my face and the boy's were on the same level. I looked into his anxious eyes.

"Yes," I said, genially, "I'm a clone catcher. Do you know where Mary is?"

He stared at me and then his mouth looked grim. "No," he said, "and I wouldn't tell you if I did. I hate you!"

A murmur of approval ran through the mass of clones.

"That's enough of that," Sir William ordered, his blue eyes popping with anger. "Clear out of here. All of you. Right now!"

Bandy legged, hands on hips, he stared them down. Slowly the groups broke up and one by one they drifted away.

Sir William was furious. He turned to Archie Three. "Are you running this compound or are you not?"

Archie Three's face hung down in embarrassment.

"I won't put up with this insubordination, Archie. Weed out the radicals. We don't want them infecting the others. We'll put them all in the 'slammer' with my crazy clone. I've spent a fortune giving these clones a paradise on earth. I want them happy in it!"

"Yes, sir," Archie Three said gloomily.

Two uniformed guards were waiting for us in the

entry hall of the "slammer." They saluted Sir William, who informed them that I wanted to visit Billy Two alone.

"He's a rough customer, sir," one of the guards said to me.

"I know that. I'll be okay with him."

"It's your funeral, sir."

"Be careful, Dunn," Sir William cautioned, as I followed one of the guards up the stone steps. "While I don't want anything happening to you, I don't want anything happening to my clone either."

"We'll both be fine, Sir William."

It was a steep, winding staircase, cold and drafty, a tower built to inspire fear. The guard and I climbed the four flights to a top room with a solid iron door. No peephole. Nothing.

"He's in there, sir. That's solitary."

"How do you feed him?" I asked.

"A food tray fits in here." The guard pushed a button and an empty tray slid out from a compartment in the door. "We put the food in it and . . ." He pushed the button again and the tray slid back in. "It can only be worked from this side."

I approved. This was truly solitary. The clone prisoner need not ever have a visit from his jailer. In a clone-compound jail, where the threat of death by execution doesn't exist (you'd be defeating the whole purpose of cloning), you use all the psychological weapons you can.

"Ready, sir?" the guard asked.

"Yes."

The guard banged on the iron door with the butt of a laser pistol. It was a nerve pistol, invented to temporarily paralyze rather than maim.

"Visitor coming in, Billy," he yelled.

He unlocked the door with a big key that dangled from a piece of wood marked with an S. He pushed the door open. The guard turned the pistol around in his hand so that now the barrel was pointing into the room.

But there was no movement from inside the cell. The guard stepped to one side. And I stepped in. Solitary was small and bare, as it should be. A bed, a chair, a toilet, and the one-way mirror-window looking down onto the compound, four floors below.

Standing at that window with his back to us was Billy Two.

"I said: you got a visitor, Billy," the guard said.

"Who is it?" Billy Two growled.

"The clone catcher," I said. "Arthur Dunn."

Billy Two turned. Those Montagu blue eyes regarded me as though I were an insect who had somehow survived a squashing.

"Didn't you have enough back there, clone catcher?"

"Not quite. I want to finish my conversation with you." I turned to the guard. "You can leave now."

The guard looked dubious. "Are you sure you'll be all right, sir?"

"Quite."

"I'll be just outside the door in case you need me. Just knock."

He clanked the iron door shut behind him.

Billy Two looked amused. "You've got guts, clone catcher," he said.

"And a few bruises," I acknowledged. "But I'm willing to let bygones be bygones, providing I get some information."

Billy Two laughed. That short, hard Montagu bark. "Beat it before I do some real damage to you, clone catcher."

"You won't hurt me again, Billy," I said. "And I don't want to hurt you."

"That's very funny," he said. "You hurt me, fat man?"

"I could break every bone in your body in less than thirty seconds, Billy Two, but I didn't come here for that. I've been hired to find Lady Kate's clone, Mary. I want to know where she's gone."

"How should I know?"

"You should know because you're in love with her. And she's in love with you. She can't be far. None of this 'gone to New York or London' business. Where is she, Billy?" I paused, leaned forward, "Or perhaps I'd better ask: which one is she?"

The blue eyes looked at me without expression. "Go easy, clone catcher."

"Not till you tell me what I want to know."

I knew he wouldn't tell me. I also had no way of threatening him to make him tell me. Clones must live until they are needed.

"I guess I'm going to have to throw you out of here, clone catcher," Billy Two said.

He came toward me. I waited. This time when he swung his fist, I caught it and flipped him over my shoulder against the wall. Before he could get up, I turned him on his back, and using a karate hold, I knuckled his cheekbone as he had done mine. He cried out. I held his arm tight.

"I'm not here to hurt you, Billy Two," I said, and let him go.

He sat up and looked at me. He rubbed his cheek. "No one ever did that to me before."

"You're only nineteen years old, Billy. When you get older you'll realize there's always someone who can do that to someone else. All right, Billy, she's around here somewhere. She's an actress. She's playing someone here. Which one?"

He looked away from me. I was striking close to a truth, and he was worried. I wanted him worried. I was going to have to use him to flush out Mary Montagu.

"I don't know what you're talking about, clone catcher," he said.

"Why did you hit me in the theater, Billy?"

He looked nervous. "I don't like clone catchers."

"That wasn't why you hit me. You might want to kill me, but not just hit me. Why'd you do it, Billy?"

I sensed his mind racing along. How much did I know? "Look, clone catcher," he said at last, "I don't know where Mary is. And if I did, I wouldn't tell you. Right?"

"Maybe. But I'll find her sooner or later."

"Later will save her life."

He was certainly right about that.

"This morning someone left a note in my pancakes. It said: 'Let her die!' Do you know who wrote it?"

He relaxed, and grinned, "You lead a tough life, clone catcher. If I were you, I'd stay away from pancakes, cereal, meats, milk, water, vegetables, . . . bread. In fact, why don't you just give up and go back to America?"

"I will after I catch her. By tomorrow I'll have her in handcuffs. Right now I'm going down into the compound to talk to all the clones I can. Tonight I'm going to Perth where I'll retrace Mary Montagu's steps."

"Don't get lost, clone catcher."

"I won't."

I knocked on the iron door. The guard unlocked it. He looked at me and then at Billy Two and at the bruise on the clone's cheekbone.

"Tit for tat, eh?" The guard smiled.

He locked the door behind us. And behind us there was silence. Billy Two was thinking hard right now. I wanted him thinking hard and then I wanted him taking action. Lady Kate didn't have much time. And neither did I.

I'd just given Billy Two his stage cleared for action.

CHAPTER ELEVEN

The Explosion

THE LIGHT FROM the gold Belgian chandelier gleamed down on Lady Kate's haggard face as she chewed a tiny piece of meat.

"Cook is to be congratulated, Alice," Lady Kate whispered. Her eyes glittered feverishly. Her plate was surrounded by tiny boxes of pills.

To her right at the dinner table sat Nurse Fitzimmons, not eating, but watching her patient for signs of distress. It was clear that Lady Kate's health ran down by evening.

I sat across from Alice Watson, who was watching me with amusement as I sniffed my food before eating it.

At the other end of the table sat Sir William, eating heartily. His plate was surrounded by Vue/Phones. A Vue/Screen hung partly down from the ceiling.

"Cook's a wonderful cook," Sir William grunted, "eh, Dunn?"

"It has the right color and taste," I said.

Alice Watson laughed. "I'm afraid that Mr. Dunn is worried someone will poison him, Sir William."

"Nonsense," snapped Sir William. "Cook wouldn't poison anyone . . . knowingly. Kate, you're looking tired."

"I am tired, Billy," Lady Kate whispered. She turned to me. "What progress did you make today, Mr. Dunn?"

"Dunn made a lot of progress," Sir William said, his eyes amused. "My clone attacked him in the compound."

"How dreadful," Lady Kate whispered. "I hope you punished him, William."

"I had the rascal put into solitary. He's getting out of hand. I almost wish I needed his heart or his liver right now."

Silence greeted that remark. Alice Watson's green eyes flashed, but she said nothing. She looked at me.

"What did you learn in the compound, Mr. Dunn?" she asked.

"I learned, among other things, Miss, that Mary Montagu was very popular with the clones. And talented. After I left the 'slammer,' where I had a friendlier talk with Billy Two, I talked to several clones. I also looked through the clone theater records. I found out Mary Montagu played many different roles through the years."

Lady Kate's eyes gleamed with pride. Her eyes were the only signs of life in her face. She was toying with her food. She had no appetite. Her makeup hardly disguised the sickly pallor of her skin.

"She got that talent from me, Mr. Dunn. Everything she is today, she owes to me."

"And she'll pay you back, my dear," Sir William said. "Rest assured of that. Dunn promises to have her in hand by tomorrow. Don't you, Dunn?"

"At the latest, sir."

"How can you be so certain?" Alice Watson asked me.

"Dunn's the most respected clone catcher in the world," Sir William said. "If he says he's certain, you can be sure he's certain—"

That was as far as Sir William got. The sound of a tremendous explosion ripped the air outside the house. The chandelier swayed dangerously over our heads. And then all the lights went out.

"In God's name, what was that?" Sir William exclaimed.

Miss Watson ran out of the room. Nurse Fitzimmons went to Lady Kate's side.

Sir William ran to the window. I joined him there. Flames were coming from the direction of the clone compound.

And then the lights went on. I could hear the emergency generators in the house working. And a moment later Alice Watson returned. She had turned them on.

Sir William pressed a button by one of his Vue/Phones. Two things happened simultaneously: the lights dimmed and a man's face appeared on the Vue/Screen overhead.

"What's happened, control tower?" Sir William barked.

"There's been an explosion inside the compound, sir. We're not getting a clear picture of it from the main gate. There's fire and smoke on the east side of the compound."

"Turn your camera on it. I want to see it."

"Yes, sir."

The man's face disappeared and a moment later the clone compound came into focus. Smoke and confusion. Clones running this way and that, yelling and shrieking, shaking their fists, and flames leaping out of a building. There were guards running around with hoses.

Sir William barked into the phone. "Get fire equipment to the compound immediately. Call Perth, if you have to." He snapped off the contact. "I'm going over there," he said to me.

"I'll go with you, sir," I said.

"And leave me here alone?" Lady Kate whimpered. Her face was a ghostly color. Nurse Fitzimmons was at her side. "I'll be with you, madame."

"And I will, too," Alice Watson said. I looked at the three women. The haggard Lady Kate, the cool and attractive Alice Watson, the calm and competent Nurse Fitzimmons . . .

They looked at me.

"I don't think there's anything to worry about, ladies," I said quietly. "The fire won't spread."

"How do you know that, Mr. Dunn?" Alice Watson asked.

"Just a hunch," I said.

"You think it was arson, Dunn?" Sir William asked me as we left the room.

"Yes, sir."

"My God," Sir William said, "I'll have Archie Three's head for this."

I looked at him curiously. Of course, he had only himself to blame.

Outside, the smell of smoke was overpowering. Dark clouds of it obscured the stars in the sky.

"I don't mind a building going," Sir William said, as we hurried toward the compound, "but if we've lost clones there'll be hell to pay. They're harder to replace than people."

"Do you have clone insurance?"

"No," he snapped. "I never thought it necessary. We ran a happy compound . . . I thought. We've had explosions in the laboratories from time to time but never in the compound."

By the time we reached the pine tree lane leading to the compound, we could see searchlights from the control towers playing their beams into the dark smoke. We could hear the clones yelling, and the sirens of fire trucks.

Sir William began to run. I ran with him.

Ahead of us a small fire truck was clanging its way into the compound. The gates had been opened for the truck, and Sir William and I ran in behind it.

"Halt!" a loudspeaker voice shouted at us.

A searchlight shone in our faces.

"It's Sir William and the clone catcher," the voice said.

In a moment we were surrounded by guards with laser rifles and nerve-gas rifles. Archie Three, holding a microphone in his hand, came up to us. He looked very worried.

"How did it start, Archie?" Sir William asked.

"Someone fire bombed the theater, sir," Archie said.

"The theater?" Sir William was incredulous. "Who was in it?"

"No one, sir. But it drew our attention. The guards came running and—" His voice broke. He looked scared. He couldn't finish his sentence.

"And what, Archie Three? And what, man?"

"And in the confusion, sir, your clone, Billy Two, escaped. Someone got the key and got him out of solitary. . . ."

Archie Three's words hung in the smokey air in front of us. They overpowered the sounds of the sirens, the water hissing against the burning timbers of the social hall/theater, the shouts of firemen, guards, clones.

"My clone is gone," Sir William repeated, dumbfounded.

"Yes, sir," a guard said. "I saw him escape in one of our guard cars, sir. He had help getting out of the 'slammer.' And as the first fire truck came in, he drove out."

"He took the road to Perth," another guard said.

"Of course, he took the road to Perth," Sir William said, coming out of his daze, "what other road could he take? Dunn, now you've got two of them to hunt down."

"I'll need a car, Sir William."

"Get him mine, Archie."

"Yes, sir."

I looked around the compound once more. The theater was burning to the ground. Nothing could save it. But the "slammer"—the jail—stood dark and empty.

Well, I'd given Billy Two his empty stage and he had taken it.

Now the hunt would be coming to an end.

CHAPTER TWELVE

Captured

THE ROAD TO PERTH was smooth as it wound between the buildings of Montagu City. But then, about ten kilometers out of Montagu City, it turned inland, away from the sea, and became the same dusty track that Norman Montagu and I had driven in on yesterday.

Yesterday?

It felt like a year ago that I'd arrived.

My headlights picked out a small sign by the side of the track that said: Perth—60 kilometers.

Sir William's solar car had an air-lift option, which meant it could fly a few inches over water or rough roads. I stayed with the wheels.

The headlights picked out rocks, burrows, small, gray hillocks, and a low scrub that seemed to extend endlessly. Once in a while a lone cabbage palm loomed up in the night—a solitary sentinel guarding vast spaces of nothingness.

Far off to my right was the sea, but I could no longer see it or hear it. Behind me, in my rearview mirror, I could see the glow of Montagu City in the sky. Only this time it was a dancing glow— the theater was still burning.

Behind me, too, the dust rose behind the car. I traveled another kilometer or two before I stopped the car and got out.

In the light of the headlights I picked out the tracks of Billy Two's car.

Then I circled behind my car and looked at the vegetation growing along the side of the track. A light film of dust was slowly settling on it. Dust that my car had raised.

A small cloud of blowflies descended about my face. I got back into the car.

I drove for another ten minutes until I came to a turnabout in the road. A widening of the track. I stopped the car just past the turnabout and got out.

A pair of glittering, almond eyes watched from atop a boulder. It was a small lizard waiting there for night-flying insects.

I squatted in the dust and found what I was looking for. Then I glanced at my watch. There was time enough, I thought. I wondered where he had dumped the car, or perhaps he had driven it over the desert. He certainly knew the land. And he was fearless.

I didn't know the land and I was not exactly without fear. Time to get going again.

The lizard's eyes followed me as I got back in

the car. I waved good-bye to it and silently wished it good hunting—one hunter to another. Now I switched on the air lift. Sir William's car rose on a thousand tiny but powerful jets.

I continued my journey toward Perth, and now the driving was effortless. Without friction. Above me hung the beautiful constellation of the Southern Cross. In its light and the light of a million other stars, I saw that I was traveling over a grassy plain— miles and miles of low scrub—whose monotony was broken only by a few dark hills to the east and the lonely cabbage palms that loomed up in the dark.

It was harsh, unyielding country, pioneered by harsh, unyielding men. Convicts had built towns, but they hadn't tamed the land. No one could do that. No man. Not even Sir William. They would take from it—gold, minerals . . . let their animals graze on it—but the land would win out in the end.

I slowed the solar craft. Ahead of me were the dark buildings of the only habitation between Montagu City and Perth—Norman Montagu's sheep station.

I turned off the car's lights and brought it to a gentle landing in some high grass just outside a sheep corral.

The animals stirred. Off in the distance I heard the braying of a wild donkey.

I sat in the car for five or six minutes, letting the sheep get accustomed to my presence.

In the glove compartment, I found a flashlight.

I put it in my pocket, got out, and walked away from the corral toward the barn. The ground was stubby, with little rocks protruding. But I found a path and followed it across a little brook and then up a hill behind the barn.

The hill I'd watched Norman Montagu climb yesterday . . .

From the top of the hill I could see Norman Montagu's house. It was completely dark. He could be asleep, he could be away tending sheep somewhere on the desert, or he could be watching me right now.

It made no difference. I had to find out.

Under the small cabbage palm at the top of the hill I found what I was looking for: freshly dug earth. There was a shovel leaning against the tree.

I squatted and picked up some dirt, rubbing it between my fingers. An indignant beetle crawled out. I dropped him to the ground.

I sniffed the dirt. Freshly turned over, all right.

A voice said: "If you're hungry, Mr. Dunn, I think I can give you something better to eat."

I turned. The first thing that met my eyes, at ground level, was a pair of moccasins. And then, looking up, pajama bottoms, a raincoat, and then an old-fashioned twentieth-century shotgun—the kind shepherds might use to scare off dingoes or wild donkeys in the Australian outback.

Above the shotgun was the rest of Mr. Norman Montagu. Only, holding a shotgun, Norman Montagu didn't look quite as mild and harmless as he had yesterday.

"Please get up, Mr. Dunn," he said.

It was clear I had underestimated him.

I rose slowly, holding my hands up.

"You wouldn't mind lowering that shotgun, would you. Mr. Montagu? It does make me nervous."

He did not lower the shotgun.

"Mr. Dunn," he said softly, "my father has given me only one job in life. To look after his sheep. We take sheep stealing very seriously here. I have strict orders to shoot sheep rustlers."

I tried to laugh, but I couldn't. He knew I hadn't come here to steal sheep. But he was quite prepared to use it as an excuse to kill me.

"I'm not interested in sheep at all, Mr. Montagu."

I had to go carefully now. Delicately. Not give away too much. That would be doubly dangerous.

His eyes were thoughtful. "What are you interested in then, Mr. Dunn?"

He knew what I was interested in. He knew why I'd been brought to Australia. Perhaps he wanted an excuse *not* to kill me. Any man who likes sheep and books is not a killer. Billy Two and Sir William, on the other hand, wouldn't have hesitated a second to shoot me if they found me poking around their land.

"I was on my way to Perth, Mr. Montagu. Billy Two has escaped from the compound and is headed toward Perth. . . ."

His face showed no reaction to the news. The world of Montagu City did not interest him at all.

"Your father ordered me to follow him. I stopped here to look at your sheep station. I saw this mound of dirt here and was curious, wondering what had been buried here."

The shotgun wavered and then lowered slightly. I breathed out.

Norman Montagu said: "A very sick sheep was buried here a few days ago, Mr. Dunn. I check its grave as often as I can to see that no wild animals have been digging it up. Whatever disease the sheep had could infect the rest of the flock."

"That makes good sense," I said cheerfully. "By the way, did you happen to hear a car go by here, going fast, toward Perth?"

The shotgun lowered some more. I stood up.

"Yes, I did," he said. "About fifteen minutes ago. I wondered about it."

"That had to be Billy Two. He's got a big head start on me. If you'll excuse me, Mr. Montagu, I'm off to Perth."

I went boldly by him and walked down the hill to the car. Norman Montagu remained on the top, watching me.

I got in the car and drove on toward Perth, checking my mirror to make sure he wasn't following me.

He wasn't.

About ten kilometers down the road, and out of

sight of the sheep station because of a series of hillocks and bends in the track, I pulled off to the side and waited.

I waited about an hour and a half, giving things a chance to settle down. Then I U-turned and drove back to the sheep station. I stopped the car about a kilometer from it, and then walked the rest of the way.

I crawled up the hill, keeping it between me and Norman Montagu's house. When I got to the top, I made sure I was facing the house.

Darkness and silence there. I didn't think I'd be disturbed again. I picked up the shovel and began to dig.

CHAPTER THIRTEEN
Old Lovebirds

IT WAS WELL AFTER MIDNIGHT when I got back to Montagu City. The fire was out in the compound, though a strong smell of smoke lingered in the air. The theater was nothing more than a few smoldering timbers.

There were lights on in all the cottages and a few lights on in the main house. No one was going to bed in Montagu City. Not yet.

As I drove past the compound fence toward the main house, a guard stepped in front of the headlights, holding up his hand.

I braked.

"Sorry, sir," he said, "but we've got orders from Sir William to get hold of you."

"What's going on?"

The guard—a young man—looked pleased with the news he was about to give me.

"Billy Two was caught while you were gone. And by the old man himself!"

So much for you, professional clone catcher, his tone seemed to suggest.

"Sir William wants to see you right away."

I pondered this news. "Where did Sir William catch Billy Two?"

"Just outside Montagu City. The darn clone was trying to sneak back in. No one knows why. I heard that the old man surprised him and knocked him out. Then he personally carried Billy Two right back into the 'slammer' in a gunny sack. A lot of people saw that. And that's where that rascal is right now. Back in solitary in the 'slammer.' And no one's allowed to visit him. There'll be no more breakouts. The clones are all upset, but there's nothing they can do about it. Billy Two's in solitary and he'll stay there till Sir William needs his body."

"Any chance of my talking to Billy Two?"

"Not without Sir William's permission."

"Well, I'll just have to get it then."

The guard put his radio microphone to his lips.

"Are you calling Sir William?" I asked.

"Yes, sir."

I gave him a wink. "I wish you wouldn't. I've got some very good news for the old man. I'd like to surprise him with it."

The guard's eyes widened. "Did you find *her?*"

I nodded.

"Hey, what about that?" He laughed. "Two clones

caught in one night. Ain't that something? That'll be a big surprise for the old man."

He stuck the microphone back in his battery belt and waved me on, grinning. I grinned back at him and drove on toward the main house.

There were only entrance and hall lights on in the house. But then the living quarters all faced on the ocean side. I couldn't tell who was awake there.

I left the car in front of the house and worked my way around to the back.

The house cantilevered out in a series of decks and apartments over the beach, the rocks, and the salty spray that rose as the surf hit the rocks.

The crashing of the ocean would provide a perfect sound cover for me as I climbed up on the rocks and hoisted myself onto one of the decks of the house.

My plan was simple. Get onto the highest rock and then haul myself up to the lowest deck which, luckily, looked like Lady Kate's.

A light was on in her apartment and some of that light spilled onto her deck.

I climbed up one large, slippery rock but not all the way to the top. The water was hitting the top. I'd have to time the intervals between waves.

So I crouched there, counting one thousand—two thousand—three thousand—four thousand—five thousand—six thousand . . . the waves were hitting at about ten-second intervals. I waited until another wave hit and then I was about to spring up when I heard noises from the deck.

I looked up. Two people had come out onto it. They were standing there in the light. They embraced. They kissed.

It was Lady Kate and Sir William.

Two old lovebirds. A sight to gladden anyone's heart but a clone catcher's.

It was a shame to interrupt them, but interrupt them I would. I made a megaphone of my hands and shouted up into the night:

"Hello, up there!"

Startled, the two figures separated. My shout caused even more commotion than that. Two more people came running onto the deck from the house: Nurse Fitzimmons and Miss Alice Watson. Why, they're having a regular midnight party up there, I thought.

"Who's that down there?" Sir William called, peering into the darkness.

"Arthur Dunn, sir."

"What the devil are you doing down there, Dunn?"

"I didn't want to wake the house, sir, by coming in the front way. And I've got to see you."

One of them shone a light down in my face. All four of them were peering down at me.

"My goodness, Mr. Dunn," Lady Kate said, amused, "you do turn up in the strangest places.

Be careful that you don't get washed away."

"I will, ma'am."

"Well, Dunn, I want to see you, too," Sir William snapped. "I've got two good pieces of news. I've captured my clone by myself. He's back in the 'slammer' for good!"

"Yes, sir. I heard that. That is good news."

"The second piece of good news, Dunn, is Lady Kate's health. And I'll let Nurse Fitzimmons tell you about that."

Nurse Fitzimmons leaned over the railing. "We've had the doctors in for another checkup this evening, Mr. Dunn. Lady Kate has made a remarkable recovery . . ." (Indeed, I thought, she must have) ". . . and they've decided she may not need any organ transplants, after all."

"Isn't that wonderful news, Mr. Dunn?" Sir William said.

"Yes, sir."

"It just makes everything splendid. Billy Two's back in the 'slammer' and Kate's going to be well. We were just up celebrating now. Dunn, in view of these developments, I've decided to call off your hunt for Kate's clone. No need to catch it any longer. Watson has your check ready. Don't you, young lady?"

"Indeed, I do, Sir William," said Miss Watson. She looked down at me. "Mr. Dunn, if you'll come around to the front of the house, I'll be happy to give it to you."

Was I imagining something, or were those cool, green eyes of Alice Watson laughing at me?

"The check covers all your expenses, Dunn," Sir William put in, "plus your fee."

"That's extremely generous of you, sir."

"I've also arranged passage for you back to New York City on the two A.M. shuttle. You've got just enough time to make it to Perth right now."

I was getting a fast shuffle all right . . . in the dark.

"I want to thank you, Dunn, for all the help you've given us."

"Thank you, sir," I said politely. "I'm delighted with all your good news. Especially yours, Lady Kate."

The old lady leaned over the railing. It was true, even in the dark, or was it *because* of the dark, whatever—her color looked better. Her eyes were gleaming.

"You see before you a very lucky old lady, Mr. Dunn."

"I can believe that, ma'am. I'm just sorry I haven't found your clone yet."

"There's no longer any need to find her. Nurse Fitzimmons and my wonderful, wonderful doctors tell me I'm good for another twenty years on my own."

"That's wonderful news, ma'am."

"Have a safe trip to America, Mr. Dunn."

"Thank you, ma'am."

They all wished me bon voyage except for Alice Watson, who reminded me to come around to the front of the house where she'd be waiting with my suitcase, my check, and a car and driver.

I told her not to rush. It would take me a while to clamber back safely across these rocks.

CHAPTER FOURTEEN

Archie Three Takes a Sudden Nap

I DIDN'T SEE the car and driver or Alice Watson in front of the house. Mostly because I gave the house a wide berth. My job wasn't over. Not nearly.

I walked along the beach until I was far from the house, and then I cut inland toward the clone compound. I found the pine tree lane and ran toward the main gate.

A searchlight from one of the control towers picked me out. A guard called down: "Who goes there?"

"Arthur Dunn, clone catcher."

The searchlight beam nibbled at my face.

"What does the clone catcher want?"

"Permission to enter the compound."

"For what purpose?"

"To check on things."

"Sorry, Mr. Dunn, but our orders are that no

one, but no one, goes in or out of the compound the rest of this night. Those orders are from Sir William himself."

"Can I talk with Archie Three?"

The guard thought it over. No one had said talking with Archie Three was forbidden, and a clone catcher was a person of some importance.

"I'll radio him, sir."

I heard him call Archie Three and, seconds later, I heard Archie Three answering. I couldn't hear what Archie Three said.

On the other side of the laser-protected fence the compound was alive, restless . . . shadowy figures moved back and forth. I knew the clones must be gathering around the 'slammer,' staring up at the solitary cell where their leader was once more a prisoner. They wouldn't be able to see him because of the one-way mirror, which would frustrate and anger them even more.

With all the restlessness inside, it wouldn't have been too hard to sneak in—set a fire, scale a fence, disguise myself as a guard. But Archie Three could let me in and prove useful inside the compound, as well.

In a few minutes Archie Three appeared on the other side of the gate in his long cape and little hat. He looked tired. The events of the night—fire, escape, capture—were enough to exhaust any clone-compound manager.

"You wanted to see me, Mr. Dunn?"

"I hear you've had a busy time of it, Archie Three."

"Indeed, we have, sir. But Billy Two has been captured and things are beginning to quiet down."

"Good. I wonder if I could come inside."

"I'm sorry, Mr. Dunn, but my orders from Sir William are that no one is to enter the compound for the next twenty-four hours."

"Why?"

"Feelings are still running very high inside. The capture of Billy Two has upset my people. Understandably. They won't go to their cottages. If you should enter the compound there is no way I could guarantee your safety. If you'll take my advice, Mr. Dunn, you'll get yourself off to Perth right away and make your shuttle back to America."

"You've heard then that my search for the clone Mary Montagu has been called off?"

"Yes, sir. Indeed, I have."

"Who told you?"

"Sir William."

"Himself?"

"Yes, sir."

"When?"

"A few hours ago."

"Do you remember the exact time?"

"No, sir. I remember, though, that Sir William called me from the main house and told me that Lady Kate was feeling much better. The doctors had examined her and decided she was not in need of any of her clone's organs. And the search for Mary Montagu was officially ended."

"Does that please you, Archie?"

"Indeed, it does, sir. As it did all the clones. We're never happy when one of us must . . . leave."

"Well, I'm glad for you, Archie, and for them. And I *will* be going back to the United States. Which is why I'm here right now. When I get back there my clients will be asking me, as they always do, what's the best kind of clone compound to stick their clones in. I'm going to suggest one like this. Thanks to you and Sir William, this is the best laid out and best managed clone compound I've ever seen. Even with the fire you had tonight, everything is normal and under control. What I want to do now, Archie, is just take one last look at a great clone compound."

Archie Three couldn't help but be pleased at these compliments.

"Thank you for your kind words, Mr. Dunn. I do my best, as you know. I hope to have the theater rebuilt in two months' time. Both Sir William and Lady Kate insist on that." He paused. "As for taking a last look about, well, I don't suppose there's any harm in that."

Archie Three gave an order to the guard in the tower. The gate swung open and I walked in.

"Would you like to see what's left of the social hall/theater, Mr. Dunn?"

"Yes."

We walked toward the burnt husk of a building, past the heart-shaped pool, and the dark tower of the "slammer." No one paid us any attention. The clones were gathered again at the base of the "slammer," looking up. Archie Three looked nervously at them.

"A remarkable job Sir William did, capturing Billy Two all by himself," I said.

"Yes. Yes. It must have been."

"You didn't see it then?"

Archie shook his head. "No, Mr. Dunn. Sir William appeared with Billy Two wrapped up in a gunny sack. He insisted on carrying him up to solitary himself. Sir William was furious. He kept saying he had to do everything himself. He wouldn't let anyone help him. It was embarrassing to me and to the guards."

"Was Billy Two pretty banged up?"

"I don't know. I didn't see him. Sir William said he'd be fine. None of us are allowed to look in on him."

"Does that go for me, too?"

"Of course, Mr. Dunn." Archie Three looked at me. "I thought you only wanted to see the compound."

"I do. But I'm just amazed at the idea of a man in his seventies subduing a tough, young clone like Billy Two."

"Sir William is an amazing man, Mr. Dunn."

"I guess he is."

We walked past some cottages, a squash court, and then, in front of us, was the remains of the social hall/theater. The smell of smoke was strongest here.

"Who fire bombed it, Archie?"

"We don't know. Sir William said he was going to investigate it personally and punish those responsible. But only after it's rebuilt. He wants to get the rebuilding done as soon as possible. Be careful where you step, sir."

A few charred metal tables and chairs were really all that was left. It was really an open-air theater now. No one was around. The attention of everyone was centered on the "slammer."

"Was anyone hurt, Archie?"

"No, sir."

"I can't even remember where the stage used to be. Was it there?"

"No. It was over there." Archie stepped in front of me to point out where the stage had been. I grabbed his left arm and spun him toward me and then before he could cry out, I pressed my thumb against his carotid artery. He lost consciousness immediately. I kept pressing. I wanted Archie to be out of the way for at least twenty minutes. After that I worked on his other artery, blocking it, too.

Then I dragged Archie under a charred metal table. I removed his hat and his cape. I found a brick and placed it under his head for a pillow—a Japanese-style pillow.

"Sorry about this, Archie Three, but you'll be all right."

In twenty minutes Archie Three would wake up with only a mild headache, but minus his cape and hat.

"Have a nice snooze, old friend."

It wasn't likely Archie Three's snooze would be interrupted. Sir William had given orders that he personally would investigate the theater fire . . . *after* the theater was rebuilt.

Nor would any of the guards be investigating Billy Two in the "slammer." That too was one of Sir William's orders.

Bless Sir William.

I put on Archie's cape and hat and headed for the "slammer."

CHAPTER FIFTEEN

Surprise in the "Slammer"

ARCHIE THREE'S CAPE AND HAT were my safe conduct pass through the compound.

As I walked by groups of clones, keeping away from lights as much as possible, they called out to me:

"It's a shame, Archie. A great shame."

I nodded in a show of sympathy.

"Someone should be allowed to visit Billy," a clone called to me. "He could be sick up there."

Again, I nodded, not daring to answer.

"It looks like Archie is ashamed," a female clone said.

"And well he should be," another replied.

By that time I was safely past them and standing in front of the entrance to the "slammer."

Through the office window, I could see two guards on duty there. One was sleeping; the other, a corporal, had his booted feet up on a table and was watching the Vue/Screen. On a peg on a wall hung the keys to the various cells.

There was no longer any point in my pretending to be Archie Three, so I took off his cape and hat, folded them both neatly, and laid them against the side of the building.

My hope now was that the guards inside the "slammer" didn't know that my mission to find Lady Kate's clone had been called off. If what I thought had happened had, in fact, happened, then there hadn't been time to notify the guards.

I knocked loudly at the door. The guard watching the Vue/Screen got up and turned the volume down on the set.

Holding a nerve gas pistol, he called out to me: "Who is it?"

"The clone catcher—Arthur Dunn."

He relaxed and opened the door. He was a beefy fellow with an honest, trusting face.

"Well, so it is, Mr. Dunn." He beamed at me. "Haven't seen you around here this evening, sir."

My luck was holding out.

"I've been out hunting that clone of Lady Kate's."

He looked sympathetic. "Ah, Miss Mary. She'll be a tough one to collect, that one. Not like Billy Two. Trying to sneak back in. The old man clobbered him himself. The rascal's back up in solitary where he belongs."

The second guard snored and shifted slightly in a sound sleep.

My beefy friend winked at me. "Jim here was

on duty eighteen straight hours. I'm letting him rest a bit. What can I do for you, Mr. Dunn?"

"I want to talk to Billy Two, Corporal. I'm sure he knows exactly where Lady Kate's clone is."

"He might at that, sir. But Sir William himself gave me orders that no one is to visit Billy Two. Fact is, I don't even know how you got into the compound tonight. It's closed up tight, I thought."

"Sir William ordered me to see Billy Two."

The guard looked at me, thinking it over, and then he shook his head.

"I'd have to hear that from himself, sir. He told me specifically: no one sees Billy Two."

That was as far as I could push it. I certainly wasn't going to radio Sir William in the main house. Not after he'd signed a check and told me to go back to America.

"Corporal, did your orders from Sir William come over the radio?"

"No, sir. To my face. After Sir William dumped Billy Two upstairs, he came into this office, standing right where you are, sir, and told me to my face. No one, but no one, is to visit Billy Two. And that's how it's going to be, Mr. Dunn."

I nodded. "I guess that's right."

I looked at the Vue/Screen. It was a program beaming in from North America. One of those ancient cowboy-and-Indian movies that the rest of the world never seems to tire of.

"Amazing," I said, nodding at the Vue/Screen, "that stuff is never seen in America anymore, but elsewhere people love it."

The guard turned to look.

I whipped my forearm around his neck and jerked his head back, sealing his mouth with my other hand. Then I thumbed his carotid. He fought back, kicking, but my thumb was full throttle and the immediate cut off of oxygen to his brain cut down his strength. In a few seconds, his kicking lost its vigor and then I let him down gently . . . unconscious. He would stay that way for at least ten minutes.

Time enough if I moved quickly. And I had to. Archie Three would be waking soon.

I propped my beefy corporal back in his chair, pulled his legs out and placed them on the table. Anyone looking in the window would think he was watching the Vue/Screen while his partner slept.

I turned the Vue/Screen's volume way up.

Then I checked the cell keys and found the one marked S. Key in hand, I started up the dark, winding stairs.

The air in the stairwell was cold and musty. The atmosphere of the "slammer" had been carefully created to frighten misbehaving clones. In a clone compound imprisonment and the threat of imprisonment is everything. There can be no executions.

I reached the top landing and paused in front of the iron door of solitary. It seemed to me I could hear shouting from somewhere. I leaned my ear against the door. The shouting was not coming from the room.

I inserted the key in the lock. When I unlocked

this door I'd either be unlocking a key piece in the puzzle I'd found here in Montagu City, or I'd be making a big fool of myself.

I turned the lock and pushed the door open. The room was dark. Someone was in there, though. Standing by the window. A short, compact, bandy-legged figure. Looking down on the compound. That was where the shouting was coming from. . . .

I took a deep breath. My fingers crawled along the wall, searching for the light switch.

Finally I felt its hard, metallic edge.

I flipped up the switch.

Light flooded the room.

The figure at the window turned.

It was Sir William Montagu. His face was bruised. His eyes were bewildered.

"Dunn," he said helplessly, "what's going on here?"

I didn't answer him. I had to be certain. I walked across the room toward him and then, backhand, I slapped him hard across his face. My fingernails scraped his flesh. My hand came away clean and dry.

He stared at me as though I'd gone out of my mind.

"I'm sorry, Sir William, but I had to know."

"You had to know what, for God's sake?" He touched his already bruised face.

"I had to know that you were you. Now we've got to get out of here as fast as we can. They'll be coming for us."

"Who'll be coming for us?"

He really didn't know what was going on. Totally confused. A prisoner in his own compound.

"The clones, sir. They're on the verge of revolt. When they find out you're in here, your life won't be worth anything."

He seemed to understand that. He gestured to the window, and to the compound below. "The world's turned upside-down, Dunn. I'm locked in here. They're shouting down there."

Through the one-way mirror-window I saw that the group of clones I'd passed a few minutes ago had now grown into a small mob. Men, women, boys, and girls . . . they carried makeshift weapons with them: rocks, sticks, cricket bats. They were dressed in pajamas, nightgowns, gym shorts, sweat suits. . . .

They had come here from every cottage in the compound.

And now I could make out what they were shouting up at the window:

Billy Two—we're with you!
Billy Two—we're with you!

"Do they think he's in here, Dunn? Don't they know that *I'm* the prisoner here?"

"No one knows that, sir, but you and me and one other. We've got to get moving before they attack the 'slammer.' They think that way they'll be freeing Billy Two."

"They wouldn't dare attack this place."

"Yes, they would, sir. They're desperate and they need their leader."

"How did he manage it, Dunn? He came into my room and attacked me. I fought back. I fought as hard as I could."

"I know that, sir. You're a fighter. Come along now."

I took his elbow and moved him along.

"But how could he get me past the control towers? The guards in there know me."

"You were in a gunny sack, sir. Keep moving now."

I got him as far as the landing. Three flights of stairs to go now and then the tricky part: to sneak through the mob in the dark and make a run for the main gate and the control towers a couple hundred yards away. The guards there would recognize us. We'd be safe once we were in their sight.

"But they know *him*, Dunn. They knew he had escaped from the 'slammer.' "

"I'll show you the answer to that as soon as we get out of the compound, Sir William."

I should have said *if* we get out of the compound. Suddenly there were the sounds of glass breaking and a door bursting open downstairs, and the clones were inside the "slammer."

I looked down the stairwell. The guards were diving out the windows to escape. They'd be running for their lives.

> Free Billy Two!
> Free Billy Two!

The shouts of the clones came echoing up the stairwell.

I pulled the old man back into solitary and closed the door and locked it.

"They're in, sir," I said.

"I'll speak to them," he said. "I'll calm them down."

"No, you won't, sir. They'll tear you limb from limb, and me, too."

The mob of clones were coming up the stairs, banging on the railing and the walls with their sticks and bats, shouting:

> Billy Two!
> Billy Two!
> We're with you,
> Billy Two!

In that chant I should have spotted a way out, but I didn't see it yet.

"Dunn, you really think they'd kill me if I went out and talked to them?"

"In seconds, sir."

"But why?"

The old man's naiveté was appalling. "Well, sir, it's one sure way to save Billy Two's life, isn't it? You won't be needing your clone's organs once you're dead."

"I see. Well, . . ." For some reason that thought seemed to calm him. He looked at me. "Dunn, you had better think of something quickly. I'm paying you a fortune."

"Not to save your life, sir. Just to find Lady Kate's clone."

"The devil take Lady Kate's clone. It's my life and yours at stake now."

That was true enough. The clones had reached the landing outside our door. They began thumping on the door with their sticks.

"Billy," one of them shouted, "are you all right?"

Idiot that I was, they were practically telling me how to deal with the situation—but I still didn't see it! The old man did, though. His eyes gleamed.

"Dunn," he whispered, "I can imitate Billy Two."

I stared at him. Of course, he could. He had been an actor and, in addition, he had Billy Two's voice box just as Billy Two had his. They were carbon copies of each other.

"Billy," the clones began yelling frantically, "are you all right?"

"Speak up, Billy."

"We'll get some powder and blow the door open."

They were getting worried out there.

I whispered to the old man: "Tell them to go back to their cottages. Tell them you have a plan to free yourself and free them, but you need a peaceful compound to make the plan work."

"Billy! Answer us! Are you all right?"

Sir William took a deep breath. He squared his shoulders. Going on stage. I closed my eyes. I wanted to hear his voice as the clones would. Not seeing the old face, just hearing the young voice—if he could make his voice young.

"I'm all right," he shouted. "I'm okay."

It could have been Billy Two speaking.

The hammering on the iron door stopped.

"We've come to free you, Billy. But we can't find the key to your cell."

I held the key up to show Sir William I still had it. He nodded. He understood.

"I've got a plan," he called out, still in perfect imitation of his clone's voice, "but I need peace and quiet to make it work. It's a plan that will close down the compound forever and free us all!"

The clones cheered.

I made a fist of encouragement to Sir William. But he didn't really need it. His blue eyes were shining. He was really young again, back on the stage, acting the part of his life. No, acting for his life. For both our lives!

"All of you, my friends, must leave the 'slammer.' Go back to your cottages. Get our friends outside to go back to their cottages. Then, when everything is quiet, you'll see me leave the 'slammer' and head for the main gate. Once there, I'll open the compound for everyone to leave."

There were cheers from the other side of the door.

"But right now you must leave this building and go back to your cottages. It's important that the guards see you've settled down."

"Are you sure you don't need our help, Billy?"

"Positive. It's a good plan."

"Good luck, Billy."

"We're rooting for you."

"If you need us at the main gate, we'll be there."

"We'll be watching, Billy."

"Thank you, my friends. If I need help, I'll shout for you."

They left then. We heard them moving down the stairs. Outside, we saw them emerge from the "slammer" and talk to those who had stayed outside. Slowly the mob broke up. Some waved toward us; all went back to their cottages as Sir William, pretending he was Billy Two, had asked them to.

Sir William and I watched silently.

He turned to me. "They believed me, Dunn."

"You're a fine actor, sir."

"They were desperate and they believed me. I hold their lives in my hands."

You always did, I thought.

"I never knew how desperate they were. I gave them such fine facilities, Dunn. Food, recreation, theater . . ." He was silent. "I've never looked at life from the point of view of a clone, Dunn."

"It's not a smart thing to do, sir, especially when you're a clone owner."

Or a clone catcher, I might have added.

"Well, Dunn, what do we do now?"

The area around the "slammer" was empty. The "slammer" itself was silent. I unlocked the iron door and poked my head out. No one was around.

"Now, sir," I said, "we get out of here."

"I'll follow you, Dunn," he said.

We went back down the winding stairs.

CHAPTER SIXTEEN

Breakout!

IF YOU GO BACK to page 67 in this book you can see on the map of the compound that it's a straight line between the front door of the "slammer" to the main gate and control towers.

That straight line is really a smooth path about two hundred yards long that ends up just about at the heart-shaped pool near the gate.

As you leave the "slammer," the infirmary is on your right and the social hall/theater (what's left of it) is on your left.

Most of the clone cottages are behind the "slammer," but you can see from the map that a few are on either side of the gate, next to the squash courts.

That meant there would be clones closer to the main gate than we. We had to catch them by surprise. Everything now depended on how fast the old man and I took off from the "slammer" and how fast the old man could run.

He and I stood behind the broken front door. The guards' office to our right was a mess. Broken windows, glass on the floor, the Vue/Screen still playing the cowboy-and-Indian movie with no one watching.

Through the windows I could see the clones standing on the porches of the cottages, watching, waiting for Billy Two to emerge.

Well, I thought, they're in for a big surprise. And let's hope the shock freezes them long enough.

I glanced at Sir William. He looked pale but grim.

"Ready, sir?"

"I hope I can keep up with you, Dunn."

"You will, sir. I've no doubt of that. Here's the plan. I kick the door open and out we go, fast as we can. Careful not to trip down the steps. There are four of them. After that, we just put our heads down and race for the main gate. I'll be with you all the way."

"You're a brave man, Dunn."

"No, sir. Not brave. Just greedy. You're my client. I've got to keep you healthy till you pay my bill."

He laughed. A good sign. The old man wouldn't choke. He'd be running with me all the way.

"I'll count to three, sir. And then I'll kick it open and away we go. Ready?"

"Ready," he said.

"One . . . two . . ." He took a deep breath.

"Three!" I said.

I kicked open the broken door and we burst out of the "slammer." We ran down the steps. Sir William was moving like a young man.

There was a stunned silence from the cottages. The clones stood there on the porches with their mouths open. They had expected Billy Two alone.

Finally one of them yelled: "It's Sir William and the clone catcher."

Another shouted: "We've been tricked."

"They've killed our Billy."

"No, we haven't," Sir William yelled back at them.

"Save your breath, sir," I grunted as we ran.

A wail of despair went up from several female clones, but now the male clones went into action. Six or seven jumped off their porches and were racing toward us.

We had a head start but they had the speed.

We had before us two hundred yards over a smooth path.

They had to cut across grass, cinder paths.

But they were young.

Behind us the compound came to frantic life again. Clones were running toward us from every direction now. At the main gate the guards turned the bright searchlights down into the compound.

One light picked us out and held us. Another picked out a group of clones cutting toward us.

A siren went off—an emergency signal to alert all guards and to alert the staff in the main house.

Sir William and I had covered half the distance already. There was only about a hundred yards left to go. The nearest clones were ahead of us on the right, veering toward us, but they were slowed down by the weapons they carried: cricket bats, sticks, stones. . . .

"We've got a good chance, Sir William," I puffed.

But now stones were being thrown at us from behind.

None of them hit us, but Sir William was beginning to slow down. His smooth stride was breaking down.

"I can't keep it up, Dunn," he gasped.

"Yes, you can, sir. You're doing fine. Just a bit more to go. We're almost there. The guards have seen us. They've opened the gate for us. Just a bit more, sir, and—"

"Ooh," he said.

A stone struck him in the back. He stumbled. I caught him and tried to keep him moving. But then a stone hit me on the side of my head. I stumbled, lost my grip on Sir William. And down he went.

The guards' searchlight held us. A big mistake. We were an easy target for more stones.

Another stone hit me as I kneeled over Sir William. I was cut and bleeding. But that wasn't important now.

"Up we go, sir," I said.

"You go on alone, Dunn," he whispered. "I can't make it."

"Yes, you can, sir."

I picked him up and heaved him over my shoulder and started once more toward the gate. Only twenty yards or so left to go, but then the gate disappeared. And I realized suddenly that what made it disappear was a solid group of clones in front of it.

We were cut off.

And surrounded.

On the control towers the guards aimed their nerve rifles, but they were afraid to fire for fear of hitting me and Sir William.

I stopped and gently lowered Sir William down. He stood there shakily, leaning on me.

"We're in trouble, sir," I said. "Cut off from the main gate."

"So I see," Sir William said softly.

The clones had us trapped. They advanced on us slowly, cricket bats, sticks, stones, and any kind of homemade weapon you could imagine . . . in their hands. In their eyes was hatred for Sir William and for me.

Suddenly one clone, a big, athletic-looking one, carrying a cricket bat in his hand, came at me. He swung the bat at my head.

I ducked and hit him in the stomach. He gasped. I chopped at his neck and down he went. I grabbed the bat.

But no sooner had I done that when I was buried in a tide of bodies. Sir William went down too.

The clones were screaming, crying, shouting, hitting, punching. . . .

I lay under a weight that kept getting heavier

and heavier and then darker and darker. So heavy and so dark that I could no longer feel their blows.

Sir William was probably dead.

I lay there in the dark nothingness, feeling nothing, hearing nothing, and my head felt surprisingly clear, lightheaded, as it floated away in the dark.

I wondered why everything had gone wrong. I'd been so close to the solution, so close to presenting my bill and getting paid. And now it was all over. And the crazy thing was: I could have been paid in full and on my way to Perth already.

Why hadn't I let them pay me at the main house? Why didn't I ever do what I was told to do?

"Why don't you do what you're told to do?" asked a voice.

I was powerless to reply. I could only agree with my guardian angel as my soul floated away.

"You break rules and now you yourself are broken," said the voice.

True, I thought. Broken so much that now I'm dead. And so what? Death isn't all that bad. In fact, it's kind of peaceful.

"You're not dead, Mr. Dunn. You can open your eyes and live a bit more."

My heart chugged. I opened my eyes. I wasn't floating through space to heaven or downward to hell. I was on my back in the Montagu City clone compound. The clones were no longer on top of me. They stood around me in a circle, looking down at me.

Also looking down at me was my rescuer. A very

disapproving Archie Three. It was his voice that had brought me back to life.

"You shouldn't break rules, Mr. Dunn," he said, irritably. "No good comes of breaking rules. I try to run an efficient compound for Sir William and you attack me and break all the rules. You've even taken my hat and cape."

Archie Three turned to the clones. "As for you, you ought to be ashamed of yourselves. Attacking Sir William Montagu. You were not brought up to hate and hurt. You were brought up to give life. Shame on you."

"But Archie," a clone said, "they killed Billy."

"No, we didn't," Sir William snapped. I blinked. Sir William was not only alive, he was on his feet. His body was bruised and cut, but he was steady on his feet. Archie Three must have got to him quickly.

"I'd like to get my hands on that young man," Sir William said. "He made me a prisoner in the 'slammer.' *I* was there. Not your precious Billy."

Your precious Billy, he'd said. But it was *his* precious Billy. And it wasn't Billy. It was Billy Two. I stared at Sir William.

"I think," Archie Three said slowly, "that we had better straighten this out now, Sir William. We—"

A rifle shot cut Archie Three's little speech short. Everyone dropped to the ground. A second shot sounded and a bullet whistled just over Sir William's prostrate form. Those weren't nerve pellets being fired but real bullets.

"Have they gone mad?" Sir William said.

Archie Three crawled over and covered Sir William with his body. Then Archie shouted to the guards: "You almost killed Sir William. Stop that right now."

A guard's voice floated back over the loudspeaker. "Archie Three, the man pretending to be Sir William is an impostor. The real Sir William Montagu has arrived here and he has given us orders to shoot anyone who has no business being in the compound."

And that, I thought, means anyone who is not a clone. Me and Sir William.

Out of the frying pan and into the fire.

Another shot went off and this one was aimed at me. I felt it nick my shoe.

"Stop that!" Archie Three yelled. "As the manager of this clone compound, I order you to stop firing immediately."

"As the owner of this clone compound," the voice of Sir William replied from the main gate, "I order you to kill the man pretending to be me, and kill Arthur Dunn, the clone catcher. They have no business being in the compound."

I looked up. Standing in the open entrance to the compound was Sir William Montagu. His blue eyes were hopping mad. With him, in her wheelchair, was Lady Kate, looking beautiful and haggard. Behind her stood Nurse Fitzimmons and Alice Watson.

Archie Three stared at the Sir William in the gate, and then at the Sir William who lay beneath him. Then Archie Three rose to his feet. "I'm seeing double," he said to himself. "There are two Sir Williams."

"No," I said, "there's only one."

I jumped up. "This is Arthur Dunn, clone catcher, speaking," I yelled to the guards. "Hold your fire. You have a Sir William Montagu there. We have a Sir William Montagu here."

"Kill him!" their Sir William Montagu shouted.

"Put your guns down," our Sir William Montagu called out. He rose to his feet. "Put those guns down immediately."

The guards with their rifles hesitated.

"Down!" our Sir William repeated.

"Shoot him!" theirs repeated.

Archie Three stepped in front of our Sir William. "If you shoot him, you kill me," he called out.

There was a silence. And then Lady Kate said quietly but clearly: "Put your guns down."

The guards lowered their guns.

"Dunn," our Sir William said to me, "do you understand this?"

"Yes, sir. And so shall you very soon."

I turned to Archie Three and the clones. "All of you, please come with us now."

"No more tricks, Mr. Dunn," Archie Three said.

"No, Archie. All the tricks are over. I hope."

I walked slowly toward the main gate. The others

followed me: Sir William, Archie Three, and practically the whole clone population.

We walked in a pool of light as though it shone down from the heavens. Though it was only the powerful searchlights from the control towers following us.

As in a theater.

When actors confront each other at the end of a play.

CHAPTER SEVENTEEN

The Confrontation

WE ALL STOOD facing one another around the heart-shaped, reflecting pool, under the guards' rifles, bathed in searchlight beams.

There were the two identical Sir Williams, Lady Kate, Nurse Fitzimmons, Alice Watson, myself, Archie Three, and all the clones.

There was a deep, awed silence, as when one sees something unbelievable, a mirage, and doesn't know what to think.

It was the Sir William who stood with Lady Kate who broke the silence.

"Dunn," he snapped, "I've put up with your nonsense long enough. You were supposed to pick up your check and be gone by now. Instead you broke into the compound against my orders."

Archie Three looked unhappy. "No, Sir William, I let him in. He fooled me. He told me he wanted to take one last look around before he left for America. Then he attacked me and knocked me out."

"Archie Three," *their* Sir William snapped, "I no longer think you're able to manage the compound."

Our Sir William snorted. I put a restraining hand on him.

"Archie Three is one of the best compound managers I've ever seen," I said. "The reason I tricked him into letting me in was that there was something wrong with your orders, Sir William. Just as there was something wrong with Lady Kate, with Nurse Fitzimmons, with Miss Watson, and . . . with you!"

Everyone looked at me now. I turned to *my* Sir William. "Do you remember, sir, when Billy Two broke out of the 'slammer' and headed for Perth?"

"Of course, I remember," my Sir William snapped.

"You told me to find him. To catch him."

"That's right."

"Where is Billy?" a clone asked.

"He's here," I said, "right in front of you."

The other Sir William knew what was coming. He tried to dodge, but I caught him and spun him around. I didn't want to knock him down. I wanted him upright in full view of everyone, bathed in the white light of the searchlights.

"You're as good an actor as your parent," I said, and ripped the theatrical mask off his face.

And there stood Billy Two, his blue eyes swiveling like twin cannons. Angry!

Sir William stared at his clone.

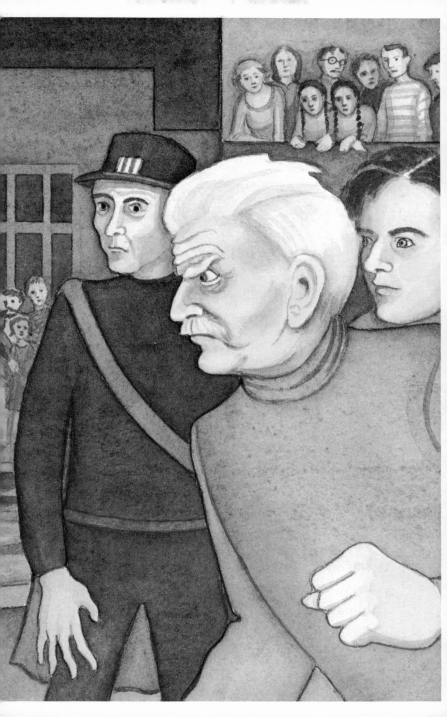

I dangled the mask between my fingers and turned to Sir William. "This, sir, was how he got you into the 'slammer.' To the guards he was Sir William. And you, in the gunny sack, were Billy Two. He fooled the guards. He fooled all the clones."

"But I didn't fool you. Is that it, clone catcher?" Billy Two snarled.

"If I let you go, Billy, will you promise to behave?" I asked.

"I'll fight you till I die, clone catcher."

"Billy," Alice Watson said quietly, "there's been enough trouble already."

Billy Two looked at the cool, intelligent Alice Watson, then at the calm but alert Nurse Fitzimmons, and finally at Lady Kate Montagu sitting in her wheelchair. They each nodded agreement with what Alice Watson had just told him.

And slowly I felt the tension drain from the clone's taut body.

"All right, clone catcher," Billy Two said, "there'll be no more trouble from me."

I let him go. He walked over to the three women. I noticed that he no longer imitated Sir William's walk.

"Dunn," said Sir William, "what in God's name is this all about?"

"I don't know when the mask was made, sir, but I think I know when the plan was hatched for your clone to become you. Last evening, after you left Lady Kate's apartment, they asked me to call off the hunt for the clone. I told them you had called me on the case and only you could call me off it. I think it must have been decided then to have *another* you call me off the case."

"The mask," Billy Two said, "was made for our play about the beginning of Australia. We needed a villainous face."

He looked stonily at his parent.

"No matter," I said, "it came in handy for real life."

"But how could he have fooled Kate? And Nurse Fitzimmons? And Alice Watson?" Sir William asked me.

"He didn't," I said quietly. "It was their idea in the first place."

The old man stared at me. All the others were looking at me, too. The clones, the women, Billy Two, Archie Three . . . looking anxious, I thought.

But it was Sir William I was concerned with now. I was worried about what I must now tell him. I decided to proceed slowly.

"I first got an idea what the plan might be when Billy Two hit me in the theater, Sir William. It was an uncharacteristic thing for him to do. It could only mean he *wanted* to get put into the 'slammer' . . . and, above all, into solitary. He had to establish the presence of Billy Two in solitary so that an escaped Billy Two could be returned there. Only it wouldn't be Billy Two returning but you, Sir William, in a gunny sack. Returned by someone who looked more like Sir William than you do. Just as you fooled the clones in the 'slammer' imitating Billy Two, he fooled the guards . . . and Archie Three by imitating you."

Archie Three bowed his head. "Sir William, I didn't know."

"No one could have," Sir William said. He turned to me. "How did you know, Dunn?"

"I didn't, sir. But I followed Billy Two's car tracks toward Perth. And I saw where he turned around and headed back here."

"But *you* didn't turn around and come back, did you, Mr. Dunn?" Lady Kate asked, her eyes flashing.

"No, ma'am."

"Why didn't you, Mr. Dunn?" Alice Watson asked quietly.

"Yes, indeed, why didn't you?" Nurse Fitzimmons asked.

They wanted to get it over with. I didn't blame them.

"For a couple of reasons," I said to them. "I wanted to give Billy Two a clear stage for action. He had to make his play and his play would lead me to Mary Montagu. Second, there was something about Norman Montagu's sheep station and his worry about it that bothered me when he first drove me here from Perth. I thought I'd just keep going and check out Norman's sheep station."

"Norman," Nurse Fitzimmons said with contempt. She and Alice Watson and Lady Kate Montagu exchanged looks. One of them was not who she was supposed to be. And the other two were protecting her.

"Don't blame Norman, Nurse Fitzimmons. You were all asking a lot of him."

"Go on with your story, Dunn," Sir William said.

I looked at him. I hoped he would be brave. He was in for a deep shock.

"I tried to sneak onto the sheep station, Sir William, but Norman caught me and held a shotgun on me."

"Norman did?" Sir William asked. He looked a little pleased. "I didn't know my son had that kind of spunk."

"He does, sir. Rest assured. I talked my way out of there and pretended to go on to Perth. Then I doubled back and found what I was looking for at the sheep station."

"And what were you looking for, Mr. Dunn?" Lady Kate asked.

"A freshly dug grave."

"Whose?"

I looked at the three of them: Nurse Fitzimmons, calm and watchful; Alice Watson, pretty and intelligent; Lady Kate Montagu, old and sick and proud, and watching me anxiously.

"I asked you, Mr. Dunn," Lady Kate repeated, "whose grave did you find there?"

"Yours, ma'am. As you well know."

Gasps went up from the clones, Sir William, Archie Three. Only the three women and Billy Two were silent.

Sir William recovered first. "You're talking bloody nonsense, Dunn. My wife is right here in front of you."

I took a deep breath. "Sir William," I said, as gently as I could, "your wife died of natural causes a few nights ago when she was on her way to Perth to attend the last performance of—"

I took my handkerchief out of my pocket and bent over and dipped it into the heart-shaped pool of water. Then, before anyone could stop me, I stepped to the side of the wheelchair in which Lady Kate sat and I began washing away the makeup on her face.

I washed away the gaunt lines around the eyes.

I washed away the wrinkles.

I washed away the sick lines.

I washed away Lady Kate Montagu.

And before everyone's astonished eyes there came into focus the features of a beautiful, proud, intelligent, young woman.

"—the last performance of Mary Montagu," I said.

A tortured sob broke from Billy Two's lips. "Damn you, Dunn," he said, "now I *am* going to kill you!"

He lunged for me.

CHAPTER EIGHTEEN

Play's End

"BILLY!" Mary Montagu's voice was commanding.

Billy Two stopped.

"You said there would be no more trouble from you," Mary Montagu said.

Billy Two turned away from me. And I was glad. I didn't want to hurt him. There was no need anymore. My job here was done. I just wanted to collect my fee, my suitcase, and leave.

I turned to Sir William, who stood there pale and shaken.

"Are you all right, sir?" I asked.

He looked at me. The blue eyes searched mine. "Is my Kate really dead, Dunn?" he asked in a small voice.

"Yes, sir. But she was not killed, Sir William. She died a natural and, I'm certain, painless death."

He closed his eyes. The suffering in the old man

made us all look away. Except for Alice Watson who came up to him. "She didn't die alone, Sir William. Nurse was with her. I was with her. And Norman was with her."

He looked at Miss Watson. "Norman?" he repeated.

"It happened near his sheep station. We were on our way to Perth to see Mary's last performance. Mary was to return with us. But my Lady's heart failed her. We tried to revive her at the sheep station. Nurse Fitzimmons can attest to that."

"I did everything I could, Sir William," Nurse Fitzimmons said. "My Lady went quickly and without pain. It was a blessed death."

Sir William looked at her blankly. And then he looked at Mary Montagu in his wife's wheelchair. And anger came into his face. "You betrayed me. All of you."

"No, Sir William," I said. "Betrayed you they haven't. Tricked you, yes."

"All right," he said furiously, "they tricked me. But why?" He turned to Mary again. "Why did you do it? You would have been freed. Your body was no longer needed. My Kate was dead. Why, Mary, why?"

"Because I wanted to save Billy's life, William, and the lives of all the others who live in this beautiful prison of yours. You still don't understand what you do when you make human clones. You don't understand that you're also making human beings

who want to live as much as you. Human beings
who will fall in love with each other. William, my
parent is dead. She had a wonderful life and a natural
death. Nothing can bring her back. But what about
Billy? I love him. He loves me. Should Billy have
to die so you can live forever? No. I say: no! No!
NO!"

Her voice rose with such commanding passion,
there was so much fire in her green eyes that for
a moment it seemed that Lady Kate was still sitting
there, not Mary. Sir William saw it, too. He stared
at Mary, and at Lady Kate still alive in her clone.

He swallowed hard. And I think it was then that
he knew what he would end up doing.

But now he said: "Child, you've tortured me. You
played a masquerade with her face and my heart."

"It's I who am to blame for that, Sir William,"
came the clear, cool voice of Alice Watson.

I nodded in admiration. I'd thought as much. Actors and actresses are wonders, but someone else
writes their lines and their roles.

"And what did you hope to achieve by that,
Miss?" I asked.

"Time, Mr. Dunn."

"Time for what, Miss?"

Alice Watson's beautiful eyes challenged me. (And
how close I'd come to being fooled by them!) "Time,"
she said, "in which to free Billy, free all the clones.
Time to put people like you out of business, Mr.
Dunn."

"And what business was this of yours, Miss Watson? You're neither a clone nor a clone owner."

"Yes, you would say that, Mr. Dunn. And, worse, you'd think that. Being a professional clone catcher. Doing a dirty job for good pay."

"Don't knock Dunn, Alice," Sir William said. "If it hadn't been for him I'd be dead. Those two—" he pointed to Mary and Billy, "—were planning to kill me."

"No, William," Mary said, "we weren't planning that at all. Clones are gifts of life, not death. Our plan was to take you from the 'slammer' as soon as the clever Mr. Dunn had gone home. We were going to put you on one of those beautiful but remote sheep stations of yours. And we planned to have you kept there the rest of your life. I know it sounds harsh, William, but it would have been a small price to pay to free all those imprisoned here. But that . . ." she looked up at the guards' rifles, ". . . is all over now."

"Now," Alice Watson said to Sir William, "you can look forward to living forever."

She pronounced it like a judge sentencing a criminal.

"You make it sound hard, Alice," Sir William said.

"I think it will be."

Sir William was silent. "I agree with you *now,*" he said softly. "I think it could be very hard." He turned to Mary. "Would you be open to changing your plan slightly?"

"I don't understand what you mean," Mary Montagu said.

"Mary, would you consider putting me on a *nearby* sheep station, instead of a faraway one? How about putting me on the sheep station with Norman? Norman turns out to be a true Montagu, after all. And if I'm on a nearby sheep station then I might be able to drop in on you and Billy and whatever children you might have. I'd try not to make a nuisance of myself. Just once in a while. A bit of visiting . . ."

It took Mary Montagu a moment to realize what Sir William was saying. Then she sprang up from the wheelchair with a joyous laugh. At that moment the lingering vision we all had of Lady Kate was gone forever. Mary ran to Sir William and threw her arms around him.

"Billy and I would love to have you and Norman visit us."

They hugged. Sir William's eyes were moist. He looked at me. "There's no point in living forever, Dunn. Not when I'll have opportunities to play with grandchildren."

But then his eye fell on Billy. He stepped away from Mary and fixed Billy Two with a stern eye. "Just the same, young man, I'm not forgiving you for banging me around like a sack of potatoes."

"I'm not forgiving *you* for putting me on earth to be a bunch of replacement parts for you," Billy Montagu snapped back.

Like father like son, I thought.

"You couldn't ever replace me," Sir William retorted. "Do you think you could run Montagu Mining Enterprises as well as I have?"

"Of course, I could. Even better. I'm your clone."

"All right, Billy Montagu, then you've got it. Montagu Mining Enterprises is yours. Montagu City is yours. And the clone compound is yours. It was always too expensive to keep up. Archie Three, draw up the necessary transfer papers."

"Wait a second," Billy said. "There'll be no more Archie Three's or Billy Two's from now on. No more numbers. No more clones. And no more clone compound. We'll take our chances with death, just as we take our chances with life. Put those rifles away, guards."

The guards on the control towers looked questioningly at Sir William.

"You heard Mr. Montagu," Sir William said. "He's in charge now."

The rifles disappeared. And so did the guards.

The clones cheered. They threw their arms around one another and began to celebrate.

"Someday," Alice Watson said quietly, "we'll see this happy scene in other compounds. All over the world."

"Perhaps," I said.

"I'm going to dedicate my life to see that human cloning all over the world is outlawed," she said.

Sir William was silent. He turned to me. "Do you think I'm a fool, Dunn?"

"No, sir."

"I don't think I ever wanted to live forever. I just wanted to run my business forever. I couldn't trust anyone to be like me. But I think I can trust Billy."

"I agree, sir."

Billy put his arms around Mary. "I love you," he said.

"I love you, Billy," she said.

They kissed.

"And so ends our play," Sir William said. "Well, Dunn, I suppose now you'll be wanting to get back home."

"As soon as I'm paid, sir."

"I don't suppose there's any way we can convince you to stay on here?"

"No, sir."

"Pity. You're an able man." He began writing out a check for me.

"Tell me, Mr. Dunn," Alice Watson said, "why didn't you accept the check I had for you and leave right away?"

"Because," Sir William said, writing my check, "Dunn is a professional clone catcher and he hadn't yet caught his clone. Am I not right, Dunn?"

"No, sir. A client can call me off any time he or she wishes. I didn't take your check, Miss, because I guessed your Sir William wasn't my Sir William, and I wasn't sure if the bank would honor the signature."

They both laughed. I didn't. Clone catching is a serious business. Only a fool would do it for nothing.

"I don't really believe you, Mr. Dunn," Alice Watson said. "But I would like to ask you one more thing. How does an intelligent person like you justify a job like clone catching?"

"It pays well."

"But to send people to their deaths?"

"They're clones, Miss."

"They're people, Mr. Dunn. Look at them."

I looked at the clones celebrating all around us. I looked at Billy and Mary holding each other. Looking at each other.

I shrugged. "I just catch them, Miss. No matter what you call them."

"You just catch them," she repeated with contempt. "You're just following orders. A cog in a machine. A link in a laser fence. Is that it?"

I felt my face turn red. The young woman knew how to get under my skin.

"Don't you see what a dirty business you're in, Mr. Dunn? Trying to reverse the natural order of things? In all of nature the old gives way to the new. And so it must be with people. There is no reason for anyone to live forever. There is no reason why the young should die for the old, in war or in peace. And, Mr. Dunn," she said, her green eyes on fire, "cloning is nothing but war waged by the old against the young!"

Sir William was holding out the check for me.

But I couldn't take my eyes off Alice Watson.

"May I ask *you* a question, Miss?"

"Please do."

"Were you hired because you had green eyes like Lady Kate and Miss Mary?"

Alice Watson laughed. Those green eyes danced. "You thought I was Mary, didn't you?"

"No. I thought Mary was you. But when I saw the two lovebirds on the deck that night, then I guessed who was who."

"I thought you knew all along, Mr. Dunn," Mary Montagu said. "From the moment you met me as Lady Kate, I thought you'd guessed the truth."

"No, Miss Mary. All I knew was that Mary Montagu had to be a great actress like her parent. And that she had to fall in love with Billy Two, as Lady Kate had fallen in love with Sir William. Clones don't have choices about that sort of thing."

"Unlike normal people," said Alice Watson, "who have choices about whom they fall in love with."

I felt myself turning red again. "I wouldn't know about that, Miss."

I took the check from Sir William and stuffed it into my wallet.

"I'll be moving along now. Good-bye, Sir William. Good-bye, Mary Montagu. Billy Montagu. Good luck to you both. Archie, farewell! My regrets for the rough stuff. And I do thank you for saving our lives.

Archie bowed. Someone had found his hat and cape and he wore them again. "All's well that ends well, Mr. Dunn," Archie said.

"By the way," I said to Billy. "I hope you'll find a job for Archie now that the clone compound is closed down."

"Archie's going to be the number two man in Montagu Mining Enterprises," Billy said.

Archie beamed.

I turned to Nurse Fitzimmons. "Good-bye, young lady. I think you're a complete professional, but you can get into trouble nursing a healthy patient."

"I'm certain you won't report me, Mr. Dunn," the competent, young woman said with the first smile I'd seen on her lips.

"Not this time."

And finally there was Alice Watson to say good-bye to.

"I take it, Miss, you were the one who slipped the note into my pancakes?"

"Yes. I thought you were a clever man and there-fore dangerous to us. I hoped to confuse you, and if not confuse you, then frighten you. I also wanted to show you how well loved Mary was. By everyone, including the cook. I thought perhaps we could appeal to your heart and make you give up your hunt. But we underestimated your dedication, or perhaps we overestimated the qualities of your heart. Nothing can keep you from your heartless profession, can it?"

I hesitated. Those green eyes were challenging me again. A woman of this caliber, I thought, could keep a man alert for many years.

She smiled and held out a firm hand for me to shake. "So be it," she said. "If you ever wish to give up your profession, Mr. Dunn, I would like to see you again."

"You make it tempting, Miss."

"I mean to. I'll need all the help I can get in trying to end the inhuman practice of cloning humans."

Sir William nodded. "And who could be more helpful than a reformed clone catcher? Dunn, a man could do worse than accept a challenge like that."

"I agree, sir."

"Think about it, Mr. Dunn," said Alice Watson.

"I shall, Miss. If ever you see me coming this way again, it will mean I'm here to stay. To join you and your cause."

"Dunn," Sir William snapped, "be human for once! Find an excuse to return."

"I'll try to think of one, sir."

"Don't *try*, man. Do it!"

At that moment Norman Montagu drove his Land Rover into the compound. Sir William and I walked over to the car that would take me to Perth.

"Well, Norman," said Sir William, "I guess you've heard the news."

"Yes, Father," Norman said meekly. "The guards have told me that you and I will be living together on the sheep station."

"Do you think you can put up with me, Norman?"

"I think so, Father."

"Then, by God, I'll put up with you. Right now, get off to Perth with Dunn. He has to catch the shuttle to America. Do you have everything, Dunn?"

I took a final look at Alice Watson standing there, watching me. She'd said she wanted me to return. A pretty, young woman like that. And me—a slightly fat clone catcher who spends most of his time living out of a suitcase. How long could a man do that? How long would a man want to do that?

I nodded. "Yes, sir. I've got everything."

The die was cast.

I turned and waved good-bye to all the clones. They were glad to see me leave, even though they knew I would never hunt one of them again.

I got into the car with Norman. And then it was back over the paved roads of Montagu City until we were on the same dusty track that led to Perth.

I waited until Montagu City was a glow in the night sky behind us. And then I confronted Mr. Norman Montagu.

"There's one more thing that must be cleared up, Norman."

"Yes, Mr. Dunn," Norman said, his eyes on the road.

"When you drove me this way last night, you made a big point of stopping at the sheep station and climbing the little hill. The hill where I later found your mother's grave."

Norman Montagu said nothing. He drove carefully.

"You wanted me to find that grave, didn't you, Norman?"

He hesitated and then nodded. "Yes, Mr. Dunn. I did."

"Why?"

We bumped over the track, a track I knew by heart.

"Mr. Dunn," Norman said quietly, "I believe in the truth. And I believed that in the end what would save Mary and Billy was the truth. I'm related to both of them, and I love both of them. I'm also my father's son and I knew that my father would not want to live forever once he learned my mother was dead. He hired you. My father always trusts what he pays for. I thought that you, Mr. Dunn, would be the best person to break the sad news to him."

"Why did you hold a shotgun on me then?"

"I wasn't sure whether you were going to dig up the grave or not. I thought that if I prevented you from trying to do it, then surely you'd come back and do it."

Norman Montagu. Timid, meek Norman Montagu! He'd only turned out to be the cleverest of us all.

"By God, Norman," I said, "you used me just as I used Billy."

"I hoped you wouldn't mind, sir."

"I don't mind at all. In fact, right now, you'd better turn this car around and return me to Montagu City."

Norman Montagu was surprised. "Why?"

"I left my suitcase there."

"You'll never make the shuttle on time if you go back for your suitcase, Mr. Dunn."

"Turn the car around, Norman."

"Surely you can buy another suitcase in America, Mr. Dunn."

"Damn it, Norman. Turn the car around!"

Norman stopped the car and slowly turned us around. "It must be a very important suitcase," he said.

"It is," I said, "very important."

Epilogue

ALICE WATSON DUNN and I now live happily together on a sheep station in the hills that Sir William gave us as a wedding present. The very one Mary and Billy had picked out for *him*. Far away but very beautiful.

Our sheep station has become the world headquarters of a movement to outlaw human cloning. Thanks to Alice's efforts and the efforts of thousands of our supporters, cloning humans has now been outlawed in the United States, Australia, Britain, France, Italy, and the Soviet Union. We're working on China, Belgium, Japan, and many other countries.

Alice and I also keep busy raising sheep. Since our first year, our flock has tripled. Alice is an excellent manager. We're making good money selling wool, though I do seem to spend a good deal of time chasing down sheep that get separated from the flock. I find catching sheep less exciting than catching clones, but more relaxing and infinitely safer.

Alice and I hope to have many children and live forever in this beautiful land.

Oops! Did I say "forever"? I meant: *a long time.* For that will certainly do.

About the Author

ALFRED SLOTE lives in Ann Arbor, Michigan, where he writes his many novels for young people. His novel *Jake* was an ABC-TV After School Special called *Ragtag Champs*. Among his recent books are *Rabbit Ears*, *C.O.L.A.R.*, *My Robot Buddy*, and *Hang Tough, Paul Mather*.

Other books by Alfred Slote

THE BIGGEST VICTORY

TONY AND ME

MATT GARGAN'S BOY

MY TRIP TO ALPHA 1

9